His Sweet

HIS SWEET
Antonov Publishing, Iceland 2018

Layout and Cover Design: Barney Black
Printed in The United States of America

ISBN 978-9935-9449-0-0

Hildur Sif Thorarensen

With love from Norway,
Hildur Sif

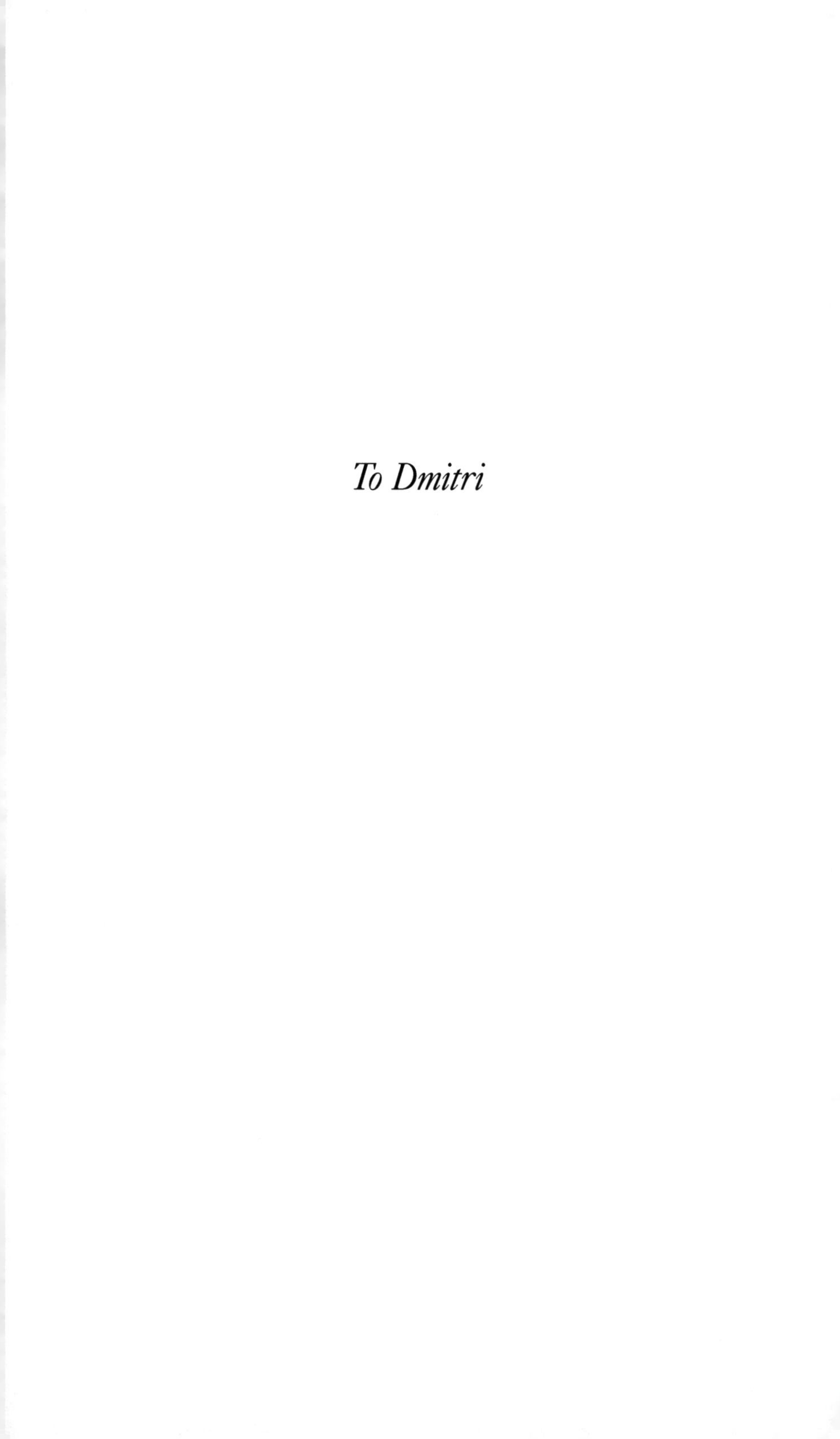

To Dmitri

I've always believed in magic. When I was young, I met a man who played the slots. He claimed he could make the spinning stop at just the right time to hit a jackpot. I was skeptical, the realist in me not ready to believe in such a talent without any evidence. Not batting an eyelid at the disbelieving youth, he went ahead and proved it, winning himself ten dollars, which was a small fortune to a kid. The man turned me into a believer, and after that I spent weeks telling everybody I had met a magician so amazing that he could even control the slot machines.

As I've grown older, I've learned how magic really works. Behind every act of magic lies a hidden trick, and none of it is ever real, no matter how much you may think it is. I didn't like finding that out. A part of me wanted to hang onto the mystical for dear life, dig my claws into it, and drag it down to my existence in order to keep it there, and with some grueling effort, I did. I kept the magic. I stuck to my beliefs even though, with time, they changed.

It was never about bunnies, large hats, or magic wands for me. I always wanted the upfront, close-up magic, not the kind that happens behind a curtain or inside a box. Card tricks were such a wonder. How could they find my card after shuffling the deck? And how did those magic rings just clink together when they didn't have any openings? I never knew, and honestly, I never wanted to know. That way I could keep believing that the magic was real.

I went to a magic show once. I had to nag my parents for months on end and do all sorts of chores, but it worked—I got my way. Dad drove me to the next town over and sat with me as we watched the mediocre magician perform his routine. I was impressed; my dad was not. He said the whole thing was a waste of time and not something a young girl should be interested in. I disagreed. Every fiber of my being disagreed. When I was tucked in bed, my thoughts gleefully drifted back to the show, and to this day they still do.

Mister Whiskers shows me magic sometimes. It's been a while since he did so, but I always enjoy it when he does. He's very good with his hands; his masterful manipulation of the deck never fails to leave me in awe. I often ask for the one where he makes my card disappear from it, so I can sit in wonderment while scrambling through the rest of them, trying to find the one I picked. On his good days, he'll do it. On his bad days, he won't.

Although he sometimes shows me some tricks, Mister Whiskers does not believe in magic. He believes in the concrete. The real. He says that there's no magic in this world, only facts. I never object to what he says anymore; I've learned from that mistake. He builds houses for a living. Says that creating something useful is the only way to go. He might be right, but if I ever got to choose, I would probably become a magician's assistant. Wear those small dresses and wobbly high heels while saying "ta-dah!" after every trick. Just like my dad, he doesn't like that idea. So I don't tell him. Instead I say that I want to become a teacher. He approves. Says women make good teachers.

Every night before I go to bed, I look at the glowing stars Mister Whiskers got me. They shine so brightly in my ceiling, though a few of them have fallen down with time. He says that's because their glue has dried up and that I'm too old to keep them anyway, so I should go ahead and take them down. I refuse, and for some reason he lets me. Maybe it's because he knows I like to look at them when he crawls into bed with me. I look at them and imagine that they're a magician's cape flowing as he walks onto a great big stage. Now I can even hold on to that thought while he hurts me, disappear into my stars and imagine I'm somewhere else. That's my power. That's my magic. That's my everything.

Chapter 1

Yolanda was feeling tired. She hadn't been sleeping too well since being appointed sheriff, but she didn't know if it was due to the pressure to perform, as she was the first mixed-race woman to serve as sheriff of any county in Alabama, or because of the warm summer nights. The heat had hit hard early that year, and she didn't want to turn on the air conditioner yet for environmental reasons. If the summer continued like this, however, she'd have to give in and do it soon.

Thankfully, the day had been slow. Solomon, her deputy, had stopped a drunk driver, but nothing else had happened to prevent Yolanda from being able to sit back at the station, answer emails, and take care of some overdue paperwork. Upholding the law in the small county wasn't really a job for two, but the incident that had led to Yolanda becoming sheriff had gotten them a rubber stamp from the governor himself, letting them run the sheriff's office with two full-time employees, along with a dispatcher by the name of June—a lovely girl in her late twenties whose bright smile somehow managed to travel through the phone lines and put nervous callers at ease.

June was the one who had sent the boys to Yolanda's desk, where they now stood staring at her with looks of incomprehension, waiting for her to examine the notebook they had brought along with them. There wasn't much to it—a black cover and looking a bit dog-eared, as it seemed to have been not only written in but also read several times over.

"So, where did you say you found this?" Yolanda asked, flipping through the pages of the worn-out book. The text was written in neat cursive handwriting, as if the author had taken great care with every word.

"Like I said, Chief, me and my buddies were just poppin' ollies by the old barn, and there they were. A whole pile of them notebooks," the tallest one said before taking off his baseball cap and fiddling with his greasy hair. "I didn't know anybody went up there, seeing it's all abandoned and shit."

"Popping ollies? Do you mean skating?" Yolanda asked, her deep brown eyes displaying befuddlement while looking the three young men over.

"Yeah. That's what I said." He stared absent-mindedly out into space and didn't seem to give his words much thought.

"What Tiny means is that we built our own ramp up there," the smallest of the lot interrupted. "No one was using the plot anyway, and Pandy here lives right next to it." He pointed at the third member of the group, who was wearing an oversized hoodie with a skating panda embossed on the front.

"Yeeee-aahh!" the panda-man exclaimed, shaking his head up

and down in agreement like a giant bobble-head doll.

"And there was more than this one?" Yolanda wasn't sure whether these teenagers were making this up or if it was real. For all she knew, they might have decided to use an old school notebook to pull a stunt on the new sheriff. Have a nice laugh and high-fives all around. Then again, none of them seemed like they had a promising career in calligraphy.

"Yeah. They were like in a box, just sitting in the back. We've got the rest of 'em in the trunk," the first one continued. "It was like somebody just dumped them there. Like they didn't want them no more."

"And why did you decide to bring them to the sheriff's office?" she continued, her eyes following their every move, waiting to catch a hint of mischief.

"'Cause of all the stuff, man. There's like creepy stuff in there, you dig?" he answered with a frown.

"So you read them?"

"Nahhh, Chief. Just that one." He pointed to the book she had in her hands. "Couldn't take any more of that shit. It's like she's locked in or something. Nasty." He shook his head in a gesture of disapproval. "Giant suggested we bring the box here, so we did. Just came straight on in from the ramp."

"And you're Giant?" she directed her words at the shortest one among them.

"Yo." He smiled, revealing a part of the grill adorning his upper teeth.

"All right." She made some quick notes on her pad. "Have you seen anybody around the old barn lately?"

"No, never," Giant answered, and the rest concurred. "Nobody ever goes up there except for us three. It's no-man's-land, man."

He was right about that. The old barn had been abandoned for years, the owners having passed away. Without any children of their own, they left the lot to the local church as well as the few animals pastured there. The animals had been sold off right away, but the church kept the plot. There were plans to build an even bigger chapel with a community hall and offices, to which the church could eventually relocate. The congregation had been saving up for the construction, and last she'd heard, they were two hundred thousand dollars away from their goal.

Yolanda remembered passing the area the boys mentioned, but she had no recollection of ever seeing a skate ramp, which meant it was a fairly recent addition. She was almost positive the church had not given them permission—or that permission had even been sought. She still decided to let things lie until somebody filed a complaint, especially since she was a keen believer that youths were better off having wholesome hobbies rather than hanging around the center of town, bothering everyday folk.

"It might be a bit secluded, but what about other skaters? Maybe somebody using your ramp? Is it possible one of them put the books there?" She squinted her eyes and chewed the tip of her pen, deep in thought.

"No way, Chief. Nobody knows about it, and we'd like to keep it that way, if you know what I mean." Giant winked at her.

"Right." She exhaled. "Is there anything else you boys would like to add?"

"Nahh," they all replied in unison, leaning their heads every which way, adding a few 'too cool for school' gestures while they were at it.

"Well, then, I'm not going to keep you any longer. You've probably got a busy schedule." Her face portrayed utter seriousness as her undertone flirted with sarcasm. "If you could just fill out this form with your contact information and show me some identification, you can be on your way."

"Cool," Giant replied, smiling wide enough to show the full extent of his shiny grill as he accepted the pen and pad.

"Solomon here will help you with the box." She nudged Solomon, who had just returned from booking his errant DUI and was taking his first sip of a fresh cup of coffee, at last finding a moment of solace only the hot beverage could provide.

The panda gentleman and the deputy trotted outside to get the box while she helped the remaining pair fill out their forms. The one with the baseball cap smelled like marijuana, and Yolanda wondered for a second whether to follow up on that but thought better of it. These young men had brought forth evidence of their own volition, and that was a big step for a crowd such as this. Underneath all that gnarliness, they might not be such a sidetracked group after all.

"Yoly," Solomon said, jolting her back from her thoughts.

"Is your name really Yolo?" Pandy interrupted, a grin spreading across his big face.

"Not quite," she replied, looking at the two of them. Each of them was carrying a big box filled to the brim with notebooks. There had to be at least twenty books in each box. Yolanda grabbed the topmost one from the nearest box and flipped through it. She then went through a few more, giving them all cursory glances, knitting her brows further as she realized that every one of them was filled out, front to back. A feeling of foreboding washed over her—those entries had all been written by the same person.

I once had a cat named Mister Whiskers. He was a mean cat. Mean and big and likely to scratch you if he was in a mood. My mom wanted to have him put down, but my brother refused. He kept guard over that cat, and it grew up to be the biggest, fattest cat I'd ever seen. Mister Whiskers was white with a black spot just above his tail. I always imagined that the spot was the source of his evil, and that without it, he would have been just a normal, boring cat. My Mister Whiskers has a spot like that too. It's on his right shoulder. I've thought about biting it off to see if that will make the evil disappear, but I don't dare. He's so big and strong, and deep down I know his evil comes from a different place.

My Mister Whiskers doesn't have any pets. He says he doesn't like animals. The cat was the same way—he always avoided our guinea pig. But while the cat didn't like anybody (not even my brother), my Mister Whiskers seems to like me and some other people too. I hear them walking around, talking and laughing upstairs. He sounds like he has a lot of friends, and he says that someday he might let me join his parties. But it's too early now. He says I'll have to wait.

Sometimes, after one of his parties, he'll bring me leftovers. I like it when he does that. Then I can close my eyes and imagine I'm there with them, chatting, laughing, and even dancing. There's not enough space in my room to dance, unless I just step in place and move my arms around. I do that sometimes but only when he's not home. Just stand there in the middle of the floor and dance my heart out.

I'm not allowed to make too much noise. If he hears me singing, he eventually looks in on me and yells. I get scared when he yells. He reminds me of an orc when he does that. An orc from one of those movies with the elves, the wizard, and the hobbits. The second one of that series was the last movie I ever saw. I'm still a little sad at not knowing how it ends. Whether they managed to get rid of that horrible ring, or if the evil eye and orc armies ended up winning in the end.

Mister Whiskers doesn't like movies. He says they contaminate the soul. That's why he doesn't let me have a TV. He sometimes brings me books, but they're seldom ones I like. It's either some autobiographies about old men, famous literary fiction, or stuffy books by a Russian author whose name I can't pronounce. There is no magic in them, only facts and information about people. I asked for the third book about the ring story once, and he got mad. He got so mad that I didn't get any food for two whole days. I've never asked for any book since, just accepted the ones he brings.

After I first came to Mister Whiskers, he gave me a book called *Alice in Wonderland*. I had been crying for days, and he said he wanted to cheer me up, to make me smile again. The book is my favorite out of everything he has ever given me. I love the Mad Hatter and the tea party and always imagine I'm there, talking to Alice and playing around with the potions. I didn't understand why he gave me this book since it speaks of magical potions and strange worlds and Mister Whiskers doesn't like that. I later learned that it's written by a famous mathematician; he called himself Lewis Carroll, but his real name was something completely different.

Like the Carroll man, Mister Whiskers wants me to have a new name. He says he's always liked Bonnie. He wants me to forget my real one and become someone else, and I pretend to do that. Pretend I have forgotten. Pretend that I'm different. That now I am enjoying our conversations about the big books he forces me to read. I even pretend to be his friend, greeting him with a smile and making him think I like his company. In reality, I'm just like Alice. I also followed a rabbit into a hole. But my hole is dark and cold, and there are no magic beings to guide me. All I have is him and these notebooks, and no matter how hard I cry and plead, this orc is never going to let me get away.

Chapter 2

Yolanda finished her paperwork, having included information in her daily report about the notebooks found by the old barn as well as details of the morning's events. The drunk driver Solomon had stopped earlier was sleeping it off in one of the three cells in the basement, and before heading out the door, she notified the night watch to give her a call once he came to.

The boxes had contained a total of sixty-five conventional notebooks, fully written out on both sides. According to her Google search, each notebook contained hundred pages, which meant they'd have to read through thirteen thousand pages if they wanted to read them all. The written entries were numbered, and the handwriting appeared to be the same for all of them.

After dusting them for prints, a skill she had gotten certified in at a detective's course some years back, she and Solomon grabbed a couple of books to read at home before meeting up again the next morning. Placing them in the passenger seat, she felt somewhat uneasy, as if she had gotten herself into a mess, one that would not let her come out unscathed.

The day passed quickly and it was nice to have been able to finish up before six and drive straight over to KFC to pick up some dinner for herself and her mom. They had been living together since Joshua, Yolanda's high school sweetheart, moved out. Seeing as her father had left when she was only a child, there was plenty of space for the two of them in her three-bedroom house.

"What a delightful smell," her mom exclaimed as Yolanda burst through the front door, holding a large KFC bucket under one arm and clutching the notebooks in an evidence bag to her chest with the other.

"Yeah. I got us a tub and figured we could just eat the leftovers tomorrow," Yolanda responded, slamming the books and bucket on the kitchen counter before making her way into the living room to greet her mother.

The older woman was a full-figured lady with curly hair and a smile that could melt away all the worries of the world. She was dressed in a wide red shirt and black culottes, her olive skin and pitch-black hair giving her the appearance of a Mediterranean fortune-teller. "Oh, that's just wonderful, darling," she said, having stood up to welcome her daughter home. "I've made tzatziki and rice that we can use as sides. You've got to eat something, Yolandoula—you're all skin and bones! No decent man wants to bite into a starved leg of lamb." She shook her head in a disapproving fashion while looking her daughter over.

"No decent Greek man, you mean," Yolanda replied, sending her mother a smug look. "In my experience, the Americans are all over the map with what they want, from Big Momma-curvy to so skinny that they can easily fall into a crack in the floor." She shrugged. "I was actually turned down for a date once because he said I had a little too much junk in the trunk."

"Well, frankly, I don't want my only daughter associating with men like that. Like I've said before, join the Greek community, darling. You'll be sure to find someone better behaved there." She gave a wide smile, displaying the slight gap between her front teeth.

As they approached the kitchen table, her mother started bringing out the sides she had made, in a variety much greater than previously mentioned. Yolanda wasn't surprised—for as long as she could remember there had always been enough food at her house for a whole starving village, which had not done her teenage figure any favors. She lethargically plucked a drumstick from the bucket and placed a small portion of her mother's delicious tzatziki sauce on the side to dip it into while absentmindedly staring into space.

"What's bothering you, honey?" her mother asked before taking a big bite of a piece of chicken, having noticed Yolanda's obvious lack of enthusiasm for the food.

"Oh, it's nothing. Just a case that came in today." Her eyes wandered toward the notebooks unceremoniously laid out on the counter. They looked so ordinary, but they were already making her uneasy.

Yolanda finished her dinner, washed her hands, and put on some white latex gloves before grabbing the top book from inside the evidence bag. Plumping herself down onto the sofa next to her mother, she started flipping through the pages while her mom watched one of her reality romances, eagerly encouraging a character to propose already. "Has Malakia hit you on the head?

Shit or get off the pot, you fool!" she screamed at the television, vigorously pointing her finger at the man standing there with a jewelry box in his hand, trying to make up his mind whether to kneel or stand.

The pages were thin enough for Yolanda to see through them. Each numbered entry seemed just like every other item in a child's diary, where you'd expect to read about boys or extracurricular activities, except that these entries were so very different. In one, she was talking about a book she had read, *To Kill a Mockingbird*, a book Yolanda herself remembered reading while still in school. She recalled profoundly associating with the narrator of the story, a little girl called Scout. It was a great book, a literary marvel in fact, that forced you to think about difficult subject matter, such as how black people had been treated in the 1930s and how far we'd come since then, yet also how little things had really changed.

She thought of her own position and what a shock it had been to the county that she, half-black, half-Greek, and a woman to boot, had been chosen by the governor himself to be the sheriff. But that wouldn't have happened without the old sheriff being caught in the line of fire and her saving his life by running towards the hail of bullets and dragging him to cover. Without her selfless act of heroism and the injuries sustained by her predecessor, she'd never have gotten the job, and deep down that made her sad. Sad for her race, sad for her sex, and sad for her nation, still hanging on to the idea that people of a certain color or gender deserved to be treated differently.

The girl writing the notebooks didn't identify with the heroine of the story as Yolanda had done, but instead with Boo Radley, the odd man who, despite being a source of fear for children, tried desperately to interact with them by leaving gifts and soap-dolls for them to find in the knothole of a tree. He turned out to be a good person, lonely but kind, and even ended up saving the children's lives in the end. The girl said that she was the same, that she might be locked in but not because she was bad, only because Mister Whiskers didn't want to let her out, and given the chance, she would have saved those kids too.

Yolanda's eyes started watering as she read the child's writings. It was as if she were fully aware of her situation, but oddly enough, seemed to be coping incredibly well. She didn't complain, whine, or write about how horrible she had it. She wrote about completely different topics—small yet positive anecdotes from her past, the books she read, or something she'd made up. As if she were using the words to distract herself from her captivity and by doing so, surviving.

As Yolanda kept reading, her mind eventually wandered to her own girl. Her sweet girl who had been growing inside her belly when the accident happened. Unconsciously, she put a hand on her stomach and bit her lip as the memory fluttered by. She hadn't been able to save her despite trying desperately, and the pain that followed had been the end of her relationship with Joshua. That fact only made her more determined to do everything in her power to save this little girl. Even if it meant using her free time to read the notebooks or swallowing her pride and calling somebody in from another county to help. It was an opportunity to make up for what she perceived as her own failure and deep within, she knew that it wasn't just about saving the girl, it was also about saving herself.

I used to have a bit of a belly, and my thighs were bigger. At one point I even had the beginnings of breasts, but they're almost gone now. Mister Whiskers says he doesn't like meat on women and wants me to look like one of those models. I don't know why. I think I look like a boy now. My chest is almost flat, and I can see my ribs protruding from under my skin. I don't understand why he likes me to look this way. I remember my dad telling my mom that women look better with some curves, but Mister Whiskers only seems to give me the amount of food I really need, and it's never enough for me to gain any weight.

When I moved in, I didn't have any hair below my belly button; that didn't come until later. He says all women should be hairless down there and makes me pluck out every single hair. I've asked if I can shave instead, but he says that shaving leaves stubble, and that's unacceptable. It's hard to pluck them out when you can't properly see what you're doing. He wasn't happy with the way I did it at first, so he gave me a small mirror to make it easier. Now I sit on the bathroom floor with my legs spread, or I kneel to get the ones in the back. The mirror really helps with getting those pesky short hairs. I remove them every day to make absolutely sure he doesn't find any on me. Last time he did, he hit me so hard my head rang for hours. I don't want that to happen ever again.

I got my first period after I started living with Mister Whiskers. That was before he began regulating my meals. Before then, I would even get Cracker Jacks on occasion. I love them but haven't had any in a very long time. I got my period a few times, and then it just stopped coming. He was furious every time he noticed it happening, so I was grateful when it went away. I still don't know why it stopped. I thought it was supposed to be there for many years, but maybe I'm different somehow.

I sometimes wonder if the pills he gives me have something to do with it. I get my vitamins every day, but now I also get some of these round white pills. He says they are vitamins, too, but I'm not sure they are. I've never seen vitamins so small. One time I got very sick with a stomach flu and threw up for days. I tried taking my vitamins but just couldn't keep anything down no matter how hard I tried. A few days later my period started again, and that's when I began wondering if the pills were something else.

I took great pains to keep it hidden that time, washing every hour and soaking my underwear to remove the blood. I was lucky because he was busy at work and didn't really come to visit all that much. Sometimes he has these big projects that don't give him time for me. A part of me is relieved, but a part of me misses him. I get very lonely in my room, and even though he gives me these notebooks to write in, they're not the same as having real company. Some days I think Mister Whiskers is all right, and sometimes I don't. They say that love and hate are two sides of the same coin, and I guess they're right. Deep down, I don't want him gone, because then I'd be alone. Without him I don't have anybody.

Chapter 3

Yolanda had been anxiously waiting for her deputy to show up to work so they could discuss the notebooks, and she jumped on him as soon as he came through the doors of the sheriff's office. Solomon had obviously slept in that morning, arriving with a bit of toothpaste still in the nook of his mouth and shaving cream smeared in his blond sideburns.

"Hey, Solomon, did you get the chance to read yours?" she inquired eagerly.

"What?" It took him a moment to catch up. "Oh, the notebooks. Yes, but I've only read some of mine. My youngest had a soccer match, and there was this little dinner after to celebrate their win, so there wasn't really a lot of time left," he responded apologetically.

Yolanda knew he loved his girls more than anything and wasn't surprised that he'd used his free time to support their sports adventure rather than putting in voluntary work on a possible case. Still, she couldn't suppress her impatience. "And...?" Yolanda took a step closer to him, pulling up her brown khaki pants by the belt as she did. "Don't hold a girl in suspense. What did she write about?"

"Oh. Um, there were some recollections from her childhood and then some contemplations about a book she was reading. I believe it was some book by a Russian, The Good Shrek or some such."

"*The Good Soldier Svejk*," Yolanda corrected and moved over to the boxes. "I've actually gotten a little farther along than you have. Some of us are obviously a bit more literarily inclined than others." She sent him a teasing look, but then she turned serious again. "The girl was describing some horrible things. Not bluntly or in so many words, but it still made me sick to my stomach. Little by little, I'm feeling more certain those laconic teenagers were right; these entries are written by a girl who's being kept imprisoned."

"What? Naahhh... You shouldn't take those fellas seriously. They're always making stuff up." He waved one hand at her while shaking his head, indicating his opinion of the youths. "What made you come to that conclusion, though?"

"Well, you see those headers at the top of each page?"

"You mean the random numbers?"

"Yes. The random numbers that increase with each entry." She pointed to three consecutive entries. She had already read those, the information burned into her memory, sending a shiver down her spine when she thought of them. "I think the numbers might signify how many days she's been held captive."

"All right, that actually makes sense. I wonder how many days each book covers. Let's see..." Solomon flipped through his notebook and jotted down the first and last numbers. "Eight hundred thirty-three minus seven hundred ninety-eight... that makes..."

"Thirty-five days?" Yolanda suggested.

"Yes, right. So there's a little over a month of entries in this book you gave me and..." He did a quick count of the days in the other book. "...just two weeks in this one. The big difference is a bit odd… how many did you say yours had?"

"There were twenty in the first one but only nine in the second. Although there were multiple ones with the same numbers, as if she was writing more than one per day. I guess it's possible her captor is only giving her a certain number of books at a time, so she starts writing in smaller letters when she's about to run out. At these points, she also seems to be trying to make them last as best she can by writing only one entry a day at most, which would explain the inconsistencies in the length of entries as well."

Yolanda watched the dawning horror in Solomon's eyes as the logic of her words sunk in. "Yikes, that's disturbing. Does she ever mention who's holding her captive?"

"No, unfortunately not. She calls him Mister Whiskers, but so far I haven't come across a real name nor anything that might help us track down her location."

"Wait, Mister Whiskers? Isn't that the name of some cat food?"

"I believe it's Whiskas, but close enough, I guess." Yolanda remembered reading about the girl's cat and wondered whether it had originally been named after the cat food. The name had then been transferred to the perpetrator, which was almost ironic in the worst possible sense, seeing as it had originally been chosen as a cute name for a fluffy pet.

Solomon's eyes grew sharp and focused, like the wheels in his head were spinning at an ever increasing speed. "She's obviously trying to humanize him by giving him that cutesy name. A coping mechanism to make him less of a threat. Does he...? You know..." He took a deep breath to collect himself. "Does he make her share his bed?"

"I think so. She doesn't go into much detail, but I'm almost positive he does. He even seems to refer to her as his wife."

"Sweet Lord of Mercy... I've got young daughters, and the thought of someone... I just..." He sounded almost lost, his eyes glazing as images plagued his mind before he quickly shook his head and exclaimed, "We've got to find her!"

Yolanda had opened one of the books and was swiping a fingerprint brush across it when she came to a halt with a gasp. She pointed to an entry labelled 857, and Solomon bent over to have a closer look, reading it out loud as he did so.

"*857 - I've been alone today. Mister Whiskers hasn't visited me once, and I'm not sure he's even home. I think it's the weekend, and he should have at least looked in on me by now, but he hasn't. He gave me some extra food yesterday, and even though I've been eating sparsely to save some, I'm about to run out. I made sure not to dance or walk around too much today to save my strength, but the bread is almost gone, and I only have one carrot left in the bag.*" Solomon looked at her, his face the very definition of appalled.

Yolanda continued, "Everything I've read is along those lines, and I think you're absolutely right—we must find her before this piece of shit does something even worse than what he's already done." She ground her teeth, knowing exactly how her deputy felt. "We have to read through every single one of these books if we're going to have any hope of figuring out who this girl is and where she's being kept. I suspect we'll need to call in some help eventually, but for now, let's dust the rest of the books for prints, put them in order, and try to find out how long she's been with that *archimalakas*."

When I was little, I used to have this yellow bunny with the softest ears. I always petted them while lying in bed, and it gave me the peace of mind I needed to drift away into dreamland. I was an infant when I got her, so I couldn't say bunny. I always said Bubby. The nickname stuck, so we ended up naming her that. When I started school, the kids got wind of Bubby and made fun of me. It got so bad that I decided to stop sleeping with her and put her on my shelf next to the Narnia books. From there my bunny could still watch over me while I slept, bringing me comfort.

One time when I was about four, Bubby got lost, and we looked all over for her. I was crying my eyes out, bawling, completely devastated. My parents called all my friends, my grandma, and a whole bunch of our relatives to ask if I might have forgotten her at their house. We ended up finding her in the car. She must have fallen out of my bag, or maybe I accidentally forgot her there, neither of which mattered because I had my bunny back.

Once when I was even younger, I refused to go to bed, and my dad was getting frustrated with me, so he threatened to throw Bubby out the window. I probably didn't believe him, so I kept protesting until, to my horror, he actually did it. He dropped my bunny out the window of our apartment, which was on the third floor of the building we lived in. I was terrified I'd never see her again; she would end up eternally lost in the big outside. When I got her back, I stopped complaining and always went to bed when I was told to.

Although I stopped sleeping with Bubby, I never stopped stroking her ears. I would always do it if something was bothering me. If I had a nightmare, a bit of petting made it better every time. There was something about the feel of soft plush against my fingers that had a soothing effect on me. Maybe it was a habit. Maybe it had something to do with conditioning, that with time, I learned to relax when my fingers stroked her ears. I never really knew the reason, but whatever it was, it didn't take away from the fact that my bunny had the power to put a smile on my face.

I read about psychology in one of Mister Whiskers' books and how you can train a rat to push a lever using something called conditioning. I've been wondering about that ever since. About whether dad conditioned me to go to bed by throwing my bunny out and whether Mister Whiskers has conditioned me to behave by threatening to yell at me, starve me, or hurt me even worse. I've tried my own conditioning experiments, attempted to setting boundaries and saying no to Mister Whiskers when he wants me to do things that I don't think we should be doing. When I try doing that, he always goes out of his way to make me regret it. At this point, I'm starting to think conditioning doesn't work on him.

Chapter 4

What's the highest number you've got?" Solomon asked from his position on the floor, where three table-high stacks of notebooks had risen, creating a tiny city of journal-skyscrapers around him.

"2042," Yolanda responded, sitting by her desk, where equally high stacks were teetering on the brink of collapse.

"1857 here," he replied and pointed at the top of his final stack. "You win—2042 days. Dear Lord in Heaven, that's an awful long time to be trapped with a monster." He shuddered.

"I've also found the first entry." Yolanda said, handing him the notebook in question. "It's heartbreaking, seeing the difference between the first and the last chapters. Her handwriting has noticeably evolved over the years. She was just a kid when she started out, unsure about how to write the letters, and now she has developed into a young woman."

"How old do you reckon she is now?" One of Solomon's legs had fallen asleep while going through the books, so he forcefully rubbed and shook it, trying to bring it back to life.

"I'm not sure, but 2042 days means she's been keeping these journals somewhere between five and six years." She skimmed over the first entry. "It says here that she's so happy to have gotten the notebooks, because now she can make a diary just like her daddy. It's as if she didn't get the notebooks right away and could have been with the perpetrator some time before the first entry."

"Well, let's look at the bright side. We at least have some idea of how old she is and when she went missing." He attempted a reassuring smile.

"Solomon, there is no bright side to this case," Yolanda responded, obviously not in the mood for any platitudes. "I've set some things in motion, called Coosa County on my way to the office this morning, and they'll be sending someone to help us out. I also called Tallapoosa and they're going to do their best to try to spare a patrolman. They've got that Scandinavian festival and said they need all hands on deck, but we'll see. I for one think this case is more important than some drunk Vikings."

"Yeah, one would think. The festival is now? I thought it was later on in the season." He took up his phone to look at the schedule. "Which was the last book, by the way?"

"This one." She handed it to Solomon, who set his phone aside before flipping to the last entry and starting to read.

"2042 — Today was the best day of my life. Mister Whiskers let me go outside for the first time since I moved in with him. It was beautiful. There were birds and grass and even the sun in the sky. It was the most amazing thing I have seen in my whole life. He said I had been a good girl the last few weeks, and this is what I get when I behave. I am so happy, and I will always behave from now on if it means I get to go outside." Solomon paused, frowning.

"It must be quite the sight to go outside after being locked away for years. I can hardly imagine."

"Right. There is something about this entry that is really bothering me, for some reason. I don't understand why this creep would suddenly let her go outside after all that time. I would think she'd have been beaten into compliance years ago, so why now?" He turned the page he was reading toward her. "See this? She even drew some azaleas and birds to commemorate the occasion. The poor thing."

"Oof, she's just so precious. It's astounding how good a person she seems to be despite everything that's happened to her." Yolanda shook her head. "But you've got a point. There's something off with this passage. Then there's the question of why he got rid of the notebooks. I'm guessing he didn't think anybody would find them up there. He probably reckoned they'd have been destroyed by the elements long before being discovered, not realizing that the back of the barn is pretty well sheltered."

"He no doubt put them there before those boys built their slide. When did they say that was?"

"About a month ago, in early May." She grabbed a calendar from her table and started skimming through it, pointing at the date she had circled when speaking to the boys.

"That fits." Solomon looked deep in thought. "So if she saw blooming azaleas that means it was early spring, maybe March or even April. So this entry is around two to three months old."

"Yes, probably. Maybe he was showing her the world because he has some sort of a plan for our girl. Something she hasn't realized."

"I've got a really bad feeling about this."

"Me too." She looked at him, her eyes a whirlwind of emotions.

I sometimes think back to the day that I disappeared. I call it my disappearance, since I think it's what my family believes happened. I was supposed to come straight home from school every day. Just walk directly home and never, ever talk to strangers. My friend Susan always joined me on my way home. She lived three houses down our street, but that day she had been away from school for over a week because she was ill.

Mom said she had something called kissing sickness and that I was not to go near her. I tried to explain that I wasn't going to kiss Susan, but she still refused to let me go. Said she knew we sometimes played dress-up, sharing lipsticks and eye shadow, and any contact with Susan's spit could infect me. I replied, "Yuck!" and remember scowling in a vain attempt at convincing her that she was simply overreacting. She still wouldn't let me, and I never saw Susan again.

That day I disappeared, I remember being very happy. I had won a prize for my painting in art class, and it was to be displayed for the whole school to see. I was just ecstatic and really excited to tell Mom, Dad, and my brother all about it. I'm sure they would have been super proud of me and even taken me out to Pizza Hut to celebrate. I was consumed in thought over what topping I'd choose for my pizza when I rounded the corner onto my street and saw a puppy on the sidewalk. He was all alone and seemed lost. I picked him up, scared that he might get hit by a car, and I was just about to take him home with me when this man came. The man was big and bearded but looked so very friendly, just like Hagrid in the Harry Potter movies.

He said he was the puppy's owner and asked if I could carry it to the car for him. I didn't know what to do. I tried telling him that

I wasn't allowed to talk to strangers and that he should just take the puppy from me then and there. He didn't want to, said he was afraid he'd drop it. I felt so bad for the little thing, he was shaking like a leaf in my hands, so I followed the man, knowing full well that I shouldn't. The man had one of those really big trucks that you need to climb up into, and he asked me to put the puppy in the passenger seat.

I couldn't reach. I really, really, really tried, but it was so high and my arms just were not long enough. Eventually I climbed up two of the steps and carefully placed the puppy on the cushion. I gave it a final pat on the head and was just about to go back down when the man's big arms grabbed me by the waist and shoved me in after the dog. It all happened so quickly, I didn't even manage to scream or kick or do anything. Before I knew it, I was inside his truck, and the door slammed behind me, almost hitting my leg. I couldn't open it no matter how hard I pushed the handle. I was petrified and started pounding on the windows as hard as I could, crying frantically and yelling for my parents.

The next thing I knew, the man had gotten in the driver's seat and told me that if I didn't stop this 'fucking noise' he'd kill the puppy. I was so scared he meant it that I stopped. I didn't dare say a word the whole time, and we drove for a very long while. I'm not sure where we went, but I remember falling asleep on the way, and when I woke up, the sun was shining and the puppy was gone. I asked him what he had done to it, and he said that he had taken it home just like he was going to do to me. He said he was going to take me home.

Chapter 5

The assisting deputy who was sent over from Coosa County was a woman in her early twenties named Tyne. Yolanda greeted her, and with practiced ease, Tyne corrected her pronunciation. She had been named after her grandma, she explained, who had always pronounced it "Tawny." Her blond hair was done up in a French twist, and the only thing missing from the very picture of a southern belle was a broad-brimmed hat and a frilly dress. She seemed nice enough, and despite having obviously gotten the job because her father was the sheriff, she also appeared very competent. After she had been with them for a couple of days, Yolanda acknowledged that her help had been extremely valuable.

"I think I've found something, y'all," Tyne said and walked swiftly over to Yolanda's table, pointing at an entry numbered 684. The young woman's jeans were tight enough to make the sheriff wonder how they didn't cut off the blood flow to her feet, but the sheriff swiftly pushed those thoughts aside to listen as the new arrival started reading.

When Tyne had finished, Yolanda mused, "You're right, this gives us more pieces to the puzzle. It's interesting that the girl mentions the trip having been long and that she fell asleep during it. That means she could have very well been coming in from another state. The question is, how far could this guy have driven in one sitting?"

"It's impossible to say. The maximum time truckers are allowed to drive in one haul is eleven hours, and that's only if they've had a ten-hour rest prior to that—but I'm guessing he wasn't on the job."

"No, probably not. Her notes only mention her dozing off that one time, so I suppose we can assume that he didn't drive for days on end. That might let us narrow things down a bit and save some much-needed time." This was likely turning into a federal case, but they didn't have anything more to go on than speculation and guesswork based on the notebooks. Yolanda didn't want to hand the case over to the government's bureaucratic mess of an agency yet, since there it was likely to end up forgotten in a dusty old file cabinet in the basement of some high-security building.

"All right then, let's start off with a believable estimate, say sixteen hours. I find it extremely unlikely that the kidnapper would drive non-stop for any longer than that. Let me just first check this one statistic..." Solomon interjected and started hammering wildly on his computer. They watched him click and clack on his mouse and keyboard, manipulating the view on the monitor like a man possessed. Time seemed to stand still until he finally let off a slightly satisfied breath. "I've just quickly looked up some numbers. There is an average of 115 children abducted by strangers every year in America. Multiplying that by the years she's been gone gives us a very large number, and since we can't really pinpoint when she was abducted, we're going to have to go back even further, just adding to the already massive pile for us to go through." He pointed to his screen, where he had opened up the statistics from the National Center for Missing and Exploited Children.

"All right, your sixteen hours sounds like a good start, but how many states does that cover?" Yolanda moved closer to Solomon to watch as he Google Mapped the distances and wrote down the states within their range. They traded back-and-forth comments on whether to measure from the borders or the middle of the states, and once they were done, she counted the final list. "That makes twenty-seven states. Well, at least we eliminated almost half of the country," she drawled.

"Yeah, but that's a good start, y'all. These cases are never easy," Tyne said. "I remember my daddy working on one of them a few years back. There was this little boy who went missing, and practically the whole county gathered to look for him. We put up fliers on every light post and announcements on TV and the radio, but despite our efforts, nothing came of it. The boy had last been seen in his family's backyard before he just up and disappeared, like the earth had swallowed him whole." Tyne shook her head as she recalled the memory. "Most people thought it was the older brother whodunit. He had a nasty temper, that boy. My daddy put the screws on him something fierce, but the boy swore on the Holy Bible that he hadn't even been at home when it happened. Turned out later that his alibi was solid as a Crimson Tide linebacker. He had been messing with some kids down at the arcade, and they had him on video, stealing a little girl's teddy bear and throwing it in the trash, that nasty li'l hoodlum."

"Who was it that took the boy?" Solomon turned away from his desk to give Tyne's story his full attention.

"We never found out. The case remains unsolved to this day. That poor boy's body didn't turn up until weeks later, and by then it had been floating down and 'round the Coosa River for Heaven knows how long. The local coroner said he had been strangled, but any evidence the perpetrator left behind was washed off in the stream. It was a real tragedy, and the family never recovered. It all ended in a messy divorce and custody battles a couple of years later." She shrugged. "Sometimes the Lord works in such mysterious ways that even the pastor can't help make any sense of it."

Yolanda smiled at Tyne's account of the events but realized that it wasn't an appropriate reaction to the subject matter and quickly turned her face somber. It always tugged at her heart strings when people could use religion in a positive way, to make sense of something so terrible. They'd say it was God's plan and therefore it would be all right. Although not a strong believer in the Almighty herself, despite her mother's hard-working efforts to turn her Orthodox, she understood the need for solace and found it a beautiful thought. What had really turned her off literal-belief Christianity was how it frowned upon homosexuals. Ever since she was a teenager, she just couldn't come to terms with discrimination against other people.

"I guess we'll have to continue looking through these pages to see if we can find some other clues to help narrow our search. Does she give any more information about the name of her school, teachers, or anything else distinctive?" Yolanda asked, just about to finish the notebook she had been reading.

"No, there's not really anything usable so far. We just have her age from our earlier approximation, but since she doesn't even know how old she is herself, it's hard to say if we're even right about that," Solomon replied, just starting to write his notes into the report.

"Wait, here's something," Tyne exclaimed in obvious excitement. "I think this is it. I'm almost sure we can use this right here..." She pointed. "It should be enough to at least narrow it down to a few people."

"What, what is it?" Yolanda and her deputy both practically surged out of their seats before crowding their new coworker.

I used to play the piano, and I was actually pretty good at it. I started learning when I was four years old and took lessons every week until the day I disappeared. I miss playing the piano. It felt wonderful to run my fingers along the keys and hear the music they created. I even used to think that someday I'd become a grand pianist and perform at concerts, and the audience would throw roses at me while applauding for an encore. That was my Plan B in case I never made it as a magician.

I was once asked to accompany the chorus at my school's Christmas concert. I practiced and practiced until I was sure I wouldn't make any mistakes. Then once we left for the recital, I realized I had forgotten to bring some of my sheet music. I said to myself that everything would be all right; I wouldn't need it since I knew the piece so well. Deep inside, however, I had doubts, and those doubts ended up getting the best of me. I started playing but fumbled and couldn't finish the last song. I felt so bad, devastated, like I had done something horrible.

Once we were back home, I was crying in my room, and my dad came and sat with me. He told me that he was proud of me, that he was so proud of all the hard work I had put into practicing for that concert and that I had done such an amazing job with the songs. He said he knew I could have played that last piece, too, because he had heard me do it so many times. He also said that even the best and most incredible people make mistakes on their journey, and this mistake meant that one day I would become something wonderful. I shouldn't be sad; I should be happy because that night I had proven I could make a mistake in front of a whole bunch of people but still walk away with dignity.

Dad had made it better. He somehow always managed to do

that. I think that's why *Peter and the Wolf* used to be my favorite children's musical and probably still is. Not because of the flute and the oboe and how we learned which sound each of them makes. Not because of the enjoyable music that came wrapped around a fairly decent story. Not because I had always liked wolves and how mystical they seemed to be. It was because of the main character and how he had been so lucky to have the same name as my dad.

Chapter 6

He looked somber, as if his whole complexion had been overlaid with a grayish hue, and his expression followed along. He attempted a smile and shifted his chair closer to the table as Yolanda entered the room, before leaning toward her and interlacing his fingers. Peter had driven directly from Washington, a whopping thirteen hours behind the wheel, in the hope of getting information about his little girl. Yolanda's suggestion of having the conversation over the phone had fallen on deaf ears; he had insisted that he needed to come.

"You said you had news. What did you find?" he asked, not wasting any time on aimless chitchat. His sorrowful eyes revealed a small glimmer of hope.

"Well, as I mentioned over the phone, we're not sure the child in question is your daughter, but since your name—" Yolanda attempted.

"Sheriff, please!" He swallowed hard, obviously struggling to compose himself. "If you've found her body, just tell me. We've been waiting so long for news that it's better to just get it over with."

"No, we haven't found a body," she quickly responded and watched as his eyes filled with hope once again. Yolanda wasn't fully up to speed on the appropriate amount to share in situations like these, so she decided to spill some of the beans; he deserved at least that. "What we did find are stacks of notebooks, written by a girl who seems to have been kidnapped. They also contained some details that may identify the girl, and we were hoping you could perhaps help us with that."

"Of course!" His response was so eager that he unintentionally raised his voice. "I'll tell you whatever you want to know. Can I see the books? Can I read them?"

"Not just yet," she replied calmly, raising her hands in a placating gesture. "My staff and I are still trying to read and analyze the notebooks, so any information you can give me about your daughter would be useful. Could you for example tell me something about her interests? Something we could use as a reference?"

He bit his lip in thought. His eyes lit up briefly as a sliver of recollection flickered into a smile. "She loved animals—dogs, cats, elephants, you name it. I often found her looking at squirrels up in the trees or crawling under bushes after chipmunks. I used to watch her playing in the yard from our living room window, and every time she discovered a new creature, her whole demeanor would change. The compassion in that child was truly a sight to behold, seeing how she tried to flatten the grass to make it easier for the little critters to travel across it."

"She sounds lovely." Yolanda gave him a gentle smile. "Could you perhaps tell me the names of some of her friends?"

"She had lots of friends. There were Billy, Donald, Oliver... she often played with the boys for some reason," he explained with a shrug of his shoulders. "Then from school there was Katie, Julie, and of course Susan from our street. I'm sure there were more; they're practically all grown up now. I see them driving sometimes and imagine my little girl there with them. Going to the mall, spending her entire allowance on clothes, and looking at boys in a way that would have my hackles rising." His eyes became damp and he shielded them by massaging the bridge of his nose.

After having read the notebooks, Yolanda was starting to get an idea of the girl. How she moved, how she smiled, the person she had become. What her father was describing could very well fit that description, but it was still too imprecise for them to be sure. Even if one of the friends' names was the same, she had to resist the urge to give anything away until they could be absolutely certain. The last thing she wanted was to bring even more anguish to a grieving parent.

"What about some favorite toys, something that might be specific to her?"

"She liked all sorts of toys and had almost outgrown most of them when she..." He trailed off, trying to find the right words. "...went away. But there seemed to be always this one toy that stayed with her and brought her joy in the direst of circumstances. When she was a baby, we gave her a yellow bunny and hung it over her crib. She was just an infant and didn't have any control of her fingers, but she still tried to poke the bunny's bright red nose. She tried every day, and before long she managed, hitting it straight on there. You should have seen the smile—she literally glowed with happiness. That's when I knew my girl would amount to something amazing. She had that determination needed to find a goal and follow through."

"Did that bunny have a name, by any chance?" Yolanda could feel her cheeks burning as she waited patiently for the answer.

"Yes, the bunny did have a name. Lily was so little when she got it that she couldn't say bunny, and it ended up as Bubby. The bunny was her friend and stayed dear to her even once she grew older. I'd sometimes see her stroking its ears, knowing that she had gotten upset about something, since she only did that if she was feeling blue. My girl was so sweet—she was the kindest soul, and I miss her terribly. We all do. She left a huge hole in the hearts of everybody who ever knew her."

"Well, sir, I don't mean to give you false hope, but the girl in the notebooks does mention a bunny by the same name. Now, of course it's possible that there are other toy bunnies called Bubby, but I'd like to think that it's unlikely. If this does in fact turn out to be your daughter, then we're going to need your help to find her, meaning that we need to know everything you can tell us about her disappearance."

Mister Whiskers calls me "My Sweet." I don't know whether he means it as a term of endearment or if it's his way of reminding me that I belong to him. He told me he's going to stop calling me that now; he says that my sweetness is slowly withering away, and from now on I'll be his old lady.

I don't know how old I really am. I didn't begin counting the days until sometime after I was brought here. I know that there have been 1152 days since I began counting, but I've been here a bit longer than that. When I was little, my mom told me how many days there are in a year. It was right after Christmas, and I was badgering her about how long I'd have to wait to get more presents. "Lily, darling, there are 365 days in the year, and it's only two weeks since Christmas. You're going to have to wait a bit longer," is what she said, and although she was probably annoyed by my persistence, she still said it in her loving voice. Those were the holidays before I met Mister Whiskers, and I guess she was right; I've been waiting ever since.

Last time I was in school, we were learning how to multiply, but I didn't get the chance to become good at it. I think it's possible to use multiplication to count how many years I have been here, but I don't know how. I figured out that by subtracting the number of days in the year over and over again I would eventually find the number of years. I got three plus some change, and since I was ten when I got here, that means I must be at least thirteen.

Math used to be my favorite subject at school. I have asked Mister Whiskers to teach me some more, but he says that women don't need to learn math, that only men have any use for it. He tried explaining it to me by saying that he is an engineer and that he uses a lot of different math at work, but he only needs simple multiplication when he's cooking in the kitchen. I haven't had the nerve to tell him that I can't even do that; I'm scared he'll get angry at me.

I sometimes wonder why Mister Whiskers thinks women should be in the kitchen and men out working. My mom worked for a big company, and she was often in meetings or doing something important for her job. I used to miss her so much when she wasn't home, but I always had Dad around, and he actually spent much more time in the kitchen than she ever did. I never looked at cooking as a woman's job, and I find it a bit funny that despite Mister Whiskers' ideas, he's still the one who cooks for me.

My dad was a carpenter, and he designed all sorts of furniture from home, putting it together out in the garage. Every time I got home from school, he would call out to me, hug me tight, and ask me to tell him about my day. Sometimes I got annoyed because I wanted to go out and play with my friends and didn't want to stay inside, talking about stuff that had already happened. Now I'd give anything to hug my dad one more time and spend some time with him.

I don't know what my mom's job was called. They told me a bunch of times, but I always forgot. I remember it had three letters, something like CBE. Dad told me she was a very important person at her job; she had a lot of power and was the one to make sure that everything ran smoothly. I sometimes imagine what it'd feel like to do what Mom did—have power, be responsible for other people's work, and always get to wear professional clothes. Maybe that's where I would have ended up if I had lost interest in becoming a magician. I guess now I'll never know. The only thing I'll ever be is Mister Whiskers' wife. His Sweet. And only his.

Chapter 7

"So, what did he say? Is it his girl?" Tyne's eyes were big as saucers while she waited for Yolanda to share the latest scoop on the case. Yolanda betrayed no emotion, keeping a cool face as she considered her response. While desperately wanting to tell them everything, she bit her tongue. She wanted more time with Peter before involving her eager colleagues.

"I met up with the father yesterday. He's shacked up in a nearby bed 'n' breakfast and is going to meet with me again just after lunch. I'm fairly certain it's his girl, but it's hard to be sure of anything at this point." She nodded toward the notebooks. "I'm hoping he'll have some information that might help us find the man who took her."

"And what did he say? Did he have any ideas?" Solomon seemed no less determined than Tyne. "He must have some theories."

"Well, we didn't go very deep into it yesterday. He gave me some details to help us narrow down whether it's really his daughter. Her name is Lily, and she sounds just as wonderful in real life as she sounds in those books. The father became rather overwhelmed when I suggested his daughter may still be alive, so we ended the conversation shortly thereafter."

"You have to tell us more—we've been working on this for days!" Solomon continued.

"Well, it's a slow start with the father. I can't rush him. This case has been in limbo for a little over seven years, and I'd like to rip the band-aid off as slowly as possible. Even though it pains me to say it," she looked at both of them in turn, "we have to account for the possibility of never finding her."

Yolanda watched their reactions swing from excited to distressed in a matter of seconds and couldn't really blame them. Of course they didn't want to think of this girl being trapped where it would take a miracle for them to find her. They wanted to believe that within those notebooks lay the key, and even though they were finished poring over half of them, the one with the answers might still be left.

"I think we'll find her." Tyne broke the silence as she stomped her boots over to the coffee counter for a refill. She had brought her own porcelain mug with her. It had the picture of an owl regally perched on a branch, a gift from her boyfriend, from what Yoly had gathered. Little quirks such as that made her endearing… the cup and the 'Fuck Cancer' bracelet she wore, which came with the story of her mom having battled breast cancer and succeeded. Tyne said she had had worn the bracelet ever since.

"I'm not so sure." Solomon had the look of pure skepticism on his face as he contemplated the situation. "I don't see how we are going to find her. We have no idea who took her, we're not fully sure who she is, and on the slim chance it turns out to be this Peter's girl, we'll sure have to hope and pray that he has kept some information secret from the police through all these years. Without that, we don't even know where to start." He rubbed his temples, momentarily closing his eyes.

Solomon was right, of course, his blunt delivery notwithstanding. It was unlikely that they would find her, but there was always a chance. Yolanda had great faith in the three of them for some reason. Their investigative procedures differed from those of the regular cops, because they were country, and country meant going your own way. Yoly knew she'd go as far as knocking on every door in the whole state if that was what it took.

"Solomon, you're forgetting something." She put on a smug look, like a card shark holding pocket aces at the final table.

"What?"

"We've already gotten much closer than the DC cops ever did. The kidnapper wouldn't have known about the barn unless he's a local, which means that we've narrowed the search radius extensively, and our chances are much greater." She knew she was right. She had to be right. "I'm sure the police conducted their original search only around the area where she lived, and that would've been no help if she was all the way down here."

"Well, yes. But there are quite a number of houses in this area." Solomon was clearly unwilling to underestimate the challenges still facing them.

"Yolanda's right," Tyne said so firmly that further debate ground to a halt. "We've got the notebooks, and I'm going to comb through each and every sentence to narrow our search. We know that Mister Whiskers—or Mister Butthole, as I prefer to call him—says that he's an engineer and that he builds houses. That right there gives us a whole bunch to work with, and I'm sure there's more to be found, just you wait." She sat down forcefully, slamming her owl cup on her desk and then delving back into the book she had been reading, taking notes as she went.

"That's more like it." Yolanda smiled in appreciation. "I really like your gumption. We should talk to the father and see what information he can give us. Then you, Solomon, might want to go down to city hall and see if they can tell you which houses have basements in them. Before all that, though, we'll have to define a search radius. I'm sure you've got some ideas in that department."

"Okay, sure. Let me just have a look at the map and give you some numbers."

"Great, then that's decided. We're not going to stop until we find her."

I missed my family a lot in the beginning. My dad was always firm with me, and it sometimes upset me, but after he was gone from my life, I started missing even his firmness. I always thought he was being strict because he wanted me to abide by his rules. It wasn't until later that I realized his rules had nothing to do with it—it was all about me. He wanted me to do well; he wanted me to be successful, and he wanted me to have the opportunities he never had.

All I thought about was magic. I wanted a cape for Christmas, a wand for my birthday, and then there were all the books and videos. David Copperfield was my favorite, and I had to see every show he ever recorded. I begged my dad to take me to see him live, pleaded even, but that never happened. At the time I thought it was unfair, but now I know that he was trying to guide me onto the right path. Toward my future.

I was an okay student but never anything special. I liked math, but everything else was somewhat of a blur for me. When I was nine, we started geography, which I thought didn't make any sense, seeing as Google Maps would take care of all my geographical needs. Then the exam came, and I did very poorly—I couldn't even name the capital of Germany. When I almost failed the class, my dad became extremely upset with me. I had never seen him like that, and it scared me. Strong emotions used to scare me terribly, but I don't think they do anymore. I have something much more terrible to fear now.

Once I was playing with my friend, and we snuck into the attic. We weren't supposed to be there, but I really wanted to show her the glittery Christmas bulb with the little baby Jesus inside. There we were, rummaging through boxes when I came across an old binder. It had a brown leather cover and papers that looked a bit worn inside. I opened it up and started reading. It was my dad's diary from when he was a teenager.

I brought the book downstairs with me, and after my parents had said goodnight and tucked me in, I'd turn on my flashlight and read an entry or two. From there I learned that my dad had loved math, just like me. He had even been the best student at his school. I also learned that he built things in his spare time—a kite, a small car, and a treehouse. He spent his time at the scrapyard looking for useful bits to use in his contraptions, and little by little, he expanded his knowledge. He even had plans to use electrical components, which included a drawing and everything.

Then came summer, and his dad lost his job at the factory. My grandparents never had much money, and my dad was their oldest, with over ten years between him and his two younger siblings. Dad wrote that he had overheard them discussing it in their bedroom. His mom had been crying. His father had said that they were on the verge of losing their house.

He wrote that he had decided then and there to give up his dreams of becoming an engineer; he would start putting his effort into finding a job. He even managed to get one, only a week later. It didn't pay much, but he gave everything he earned to his parents. The job was a carpenter's assistant and he ended up taking night courses in carpentry, eventually graduating as a master in the field.

His parents kept the house. It's the house where I always used to visit them, and I really love it. Finding the book helped me understand what dad's plan was all along. He was trying to give me the world, but all I wanted was magic. That's what upset him—not the fact I had an interest in something but the fact that I wasn't putting in the effort toward my future. He was too proud to tell me about his past, but I was glad I knew. It really set me straight, and I never came close to failing ever again. I'm sure I'd have become something great. Something dad would have been proud of. If it hadn't been for Mister Whiskers, I would have. I'm sure I would have.

Chapter 8

The father looked much better the day after; he had obviously showered, shaved, and caught some shut-eye. He had brought a large, blue Walmart bag with him, one of those reusable bags of materials that are made to last and support heavy groceries. From her position, Yolanda couldn't see what he had in the bag, but it looked heavy and square-shaped, as if it were bricks from the Yellow Brick Road. She was half expecting to see Dorothy come trailing along behind him.

As this was to be a formal interview, she brought Solomon in with her and asked him to record it so they could have easy access to the information after Peter's departure. Lily's father gave his assent with a shrug before slamming his Walmart bag onto the table and emptying its contents.

It contained mountains of information. Articles, pictures, videotapes, and every other piece of documentation that might have accumulated over the years after a person's disappearance. The father had obviously never even tried to get on with his life, instead devoting himself to the search, keeping the case open as long as he possibly could after the police had stepped away from it.

"Alrighty, I see you've got a mountain of media with you," Yolanda said, bemused at his efforts to straighten out the newly made mess on the table.

"Yes. This is every single news interview caught on camera that was related to the case, and these are the radio interviews." He pointed at two boxes with VHS tapes as well as some cassettes. "Those vultures don't miss a thing, so I decided that keeping them could come in handy, as they might be worth another look."

"That's very smart thinking. There's never too much evidence," she replied, opening one of the boxes and finding nine VHS tapes inside, neatly labelled by date and subject.

"Then these are the news articles. There were interviews with all sorts of people—her classmates, our neighbors, and of course everyone in the family was taken in for their fifteen minutes. There was even a time when people..." he hesitated, loosening his tie and clearing his throat, "...a time when people thought I had done it... had killed her... killed my baby girl." A tear started maturing in his eye, and he opened them both wide before swiftly brushing it away with the tips of his fingers, trying to keep his composure.

"Well, those voices will now be put to sleep." Yolanda considered placing her hand on his in a comforting gesture but thought better of it; she didn't really know the man. "And what is the third pile?"

"That's the police documents." He looked a bit abashed, as if unsure whether to share that particular piece of information or not.

"I know it's not procedure or legal, for that matter, for me to have them, but I've got a buddy in the force, and he gave me a copy when it became clear that the police seemed to have completely forgotten about my Lily."

"Gave you a copy?" Solomon had stopped taking notes and stared at the man in surprise.

"Yeah... Look, I don't want him to get in hot water for this; he was just being a friend. I wouldn't even have told you if I didn't... if I didn't think it could help, and... I just really want to find my baby." His eyes were pleading, and Yolanda knew that she wouldn't even dream of causing more trouble to this man. She was certain Solomon wouldn't go above her head, so this piece of information was to remain between the three of them.

"Who was in charge of your case up there?" Yolanda asked as she started skimming through the police reports from the top of the pile.

"Detective Rick Matthews was lead detective." He paused for a moment to scramble through some papers. "Here's their contact information. The FBI got involved pretty quickly, though, and we had our own contact over there. Her name was Rachel Philips, and you should have her details right there."

"Great, I'm going to have Deputy Tyne take copies of all these files, if you don't mind."

"No, of course not."

As Yolanda gathered the papers, she contemplated the situation. Now that they could be quite sure who the girl was, and since there was already an open case on her disappearance, she knew she'd have to contact the police department up in DC as well as the FBI. A part of her didn't want to get others involved; she wanted to be the one to save that girl. Not because of the credit or the fame that would come with it, but rather because she needed to prove to herself that she could, that she wasn't useless.

Suddenly Tyne barged in, her blue eyes looking even bigger and more vibrant than before. She was clutching a piece of paper in one hand, nudging Yolanda to come talk to her.

"What, what is it?" Yolanda asked once they'd huddled together a short distance from the meeting room.

"I found somebody," she breathlessly replied, showing Yoly a felon's rap sheet. "He was convicted in 1990 for child abuse but got out in 2000. He lives over by Jordan Lake—and get this, he's been working for the big truck company down in Montgomery."

"A big truck with steps," Yolanda replied, her face taking on a stunned expression as the significance hit her. "Let's go talk to him, but we'd better bring Solomon along in case this turns out to be our guy. I have a feeling he won't make it easy for us."

It's vacation time. Mister Whiskers says it'll be Christmas soon, and that means I might get some nice food to eat. His company always gives him a large ham, cheeses, and other nice things for the holidays, and sometimes he'll even share some of it with me. I love it when he gives me Christmas food. I tend to keep it for a few days so I can enjoy it longer.

I asked him for a Christmas present once. I really wanted an orange hoodie, one that was soft. He said I was too big for presents and that he wasn't going to participate in such stupid religious traditions. He said that Christmas was the winter solstice and that it had nothing to do with Christianity or Jesus. I didn't want to tell him that I believed the little baby Jesus was born to help us be better people; I knew if I did, it would make him crazy. He doesn't even believe in God.

For some reason, Mister Whiskers has been very mad these past few days, much more than normal. He's always angry, yelling, or telling me off, and it seems like I can never do anything right. I know I don't always understand what he wants from me, and sometimes I make mistakes, but this is different. It's like something is wrong, and I don't think it's me.

Yesterday I asked him if everything was okay, and at first he didn't answer, but then he just yelled again. He told me it was none of my business and that I shouldn't ask questions like that. Curiosity kills cats and nosy girls, he said. I instantly shut my mouth and remained very quiet, not looking him in the eye. I've learned that it's usually the best way to stop him from hitting me when he's mad like that, but he did so anyway. He threw me into the wall, and I really hurt my back. I've been in so much pain since last night that I was only able to fall asleep lying on my side.

I don't know if he'll visit me today, but I'm hoping he doesn't come until he's feeling better. Maybe he's just angry at Christmas and the people celebrating. This is the first time he is, though, so I'm not so sure that's the reason. Whatever it is, it's making me scared. Scared he'll come back to hurt me more. Scared he'll come back even angrier. Scared if I say the wrong thing, he'll do something even worse

Chapter 9

The trucker's name was Jacob Price, and he had been working for Transporticon for over a decade, or ever since he got out of prison. According to his employer, he was always on time and did a good job. No complaints during the entire time he had worked there.

In order not to spook his boss, Yolanda had mentioned that he could have been a witness and could help with an ongoing investigation. The boss had then offered the information that Jacob had the next two days off, and it should be easy to catch him at home.

"Do you think he's our guy?" Solomon asked while examining the trucker's house from the outside.

"I'm not sure. We'll have to talk to him to try and figure it out," Yolanda responded as she examined the surroundings.

Mr. Price lived in a one-story ranch painted light blue with white window frames and a neat gray roof. The grass was meticulously groomed, and it all looked very well maintained, as if the owner took great care of his property. The only thing missing from the picture of a perfect home was the white picket fence and a happy little dog rolling around on the front lawn. As they looked about, there was a lone mailbox by the pavement and a Nissan Leaf charging in front of the garage.

"This house looks almost too neat," Solomon said as he turned the corner to check out the rest of the property. He had hardly finished his sentence when the door opened, and a man in his forties came out, his face showing utter puzzlement.

"Who are you, and what are you doing on my property?" the man said, putting on his glasses to make out Yolanda's uniform. "Are you the sheriff? What's going on?" He stepped out of the house, coming closer to Yoly, who stood in the middle of his lawn.

She quickly approached him, putting on a grand smile. "My name is Yolanda, and I'm the sheriff from over in Crowswood. This here is Solomon, my deputy." The man shook their hands. "You must be Mr. Jacob Price?"

"Yes, I am. How can I help you?"

"Would you mind if we came in for a second?"

"Of course not. Please, follow me," he said and directed them inside the house to the living room. "Can I get you anything? Coffee? Tea?"

"No, thank you. We're fine." They had a policy of never accepting any drinks from persons of interest. There had been some cases of spiked drinks in other counties and nearby states, and since then, Yolanda had decided it was better to be safe than sorry.

Mr. Price disappeared into the kitchen for a minute and came back with a mug of newly brewed coffee. "I hope you don't mind if I have a cup. I slept in today and haven't had any yet; I was working on my models well into the night."

"Models?" Solomon repeated, curious.

"Yes, I like to build models in my spare time. It's a bit of a hobby of mine. Let me show you." He stood up and fetched a giant Viking long ship, extremely detailed and painted to perfection.

"Whoa, that's amazing," Solomon exclaimed and got up from his seat to take a better look. "You made that?"

"Yes. This is what I was working on last night. I'm such a big fan of history that I try to get my hands on models that display some interesting parts of it, the Viking era being one of my favorites." He smiled, and to Yoly's surprise, his smile was very warm and inviting.

"How long did it take you to finish it?" Solomon was completely mesmerized by the ship, and Yolanda wondered how long it would take him to touch one of the pieces and accidentally break it off. To her relief, he knew better than to put his clumsy fingers anywhere near it.

"Oh, I'd say about ten days. I had a few long shifts, so I couldn't attend to it every day, but it was more or less every moment that I wasn't at work." He stroked his hand against the ship's hull. "Now, what can I do for you good folk?" He placed the ship on the living room table and sat down across from them.

"We're working on a missing person's case," Yoly started and withdrew a picture of Lily and handed it to Jacob. He accepted and scrutinized it, wrinkling his forehead and turning his head sideways in order to try to view it from every angle. "This girl has been missing for some time now, and we're asking around, trying to figure out if anybody knows anything."

"I'm sorry... I don't think I know her." He placed the photo back on the table, still turning it toward him and directing his eyes toward it every now and then. "I'm not sure why, but there's something familiar about her face, but I just can't place it."

"I understand. This is not the most recent picture, so if you manage to remember something, please give us a call." Yoly handed him her card.

"Of course. Can I hold on to the picture?" he asked, his eyes emanating pure innocence.

Yoly wanted to say yes, but given this guy's background, she just didn't feel right letting him have the picture, not knowing what he'd use it for. That little girl had gone through more than enough. "I'm sorry, but we only have this one," she replied, and he nodded in understanding.

"Oh, I know." He whipped out his mobile phone, and before Yolanda could get in a word of protest, he had taken a picture of the photo. "There we are; now I can perhaps come up with something once I've cleared my head." He looked proud, like a child showing his parents what a good job he had done.

"Yeah, I guess that's all right," she replied hesitantly, letting the moment of silence drag on, knowing that she had to get to the main reason for their visit. "I don't mean to be rude, but I'm aware of your prison sentence and was wondering if you could tell me a little bit about that."

His face turned grim as his shoulders sank dejectedly and he leaned back into the sofa, creating as much distance between the two of them as he could. "I'm never going to be allowed to escape that, am I?" His tone made it evident that she had struck a nerve.

"To be clear, I'm not accusing you of anything. It's just procedure to talk to anybody who..."

"Who has ever been convicted of a sex crime," he finished for her, shaking his head. "It's true, I was convicted, but it's not the way you think." He buried his face in his hands and slid them down toward his chin while blowing hard through his nose.

"Could you elaborate?" Yolanda had taken out her pad and started taking notes.

"I'm forty-one years old, and I sat in prison from the age of twenty-one until the day I turned thirty-four," he started. "Nobody ever came to visit me in prison. My own mother didn't want to look at me, her 'pedophile' son. And do you know why I sat in prison for so long? Why I lost the best years of my life?" He didn't wait for an answer. "It was because of a girl."

"A girl?" Yolanda hadn't given herself time to read up on the case and now regretted it. She was so focused on getting Lily out of the hands of Mister Whiskers that she had run out the door as soon as they had a suspect, ready for a harsh interrogation.

"Yes, a girl. We were in love."

"I don't understand how that has anything to do with your sentence." Yolanda had stopped writing and was now giving him all her attention to show respect for his story.

"Well... when I turned twenty-one, I went out to celebrate with my buddies. A night I've regretted ever since." Price didn't seem angry but rather saddened by his story. "The guys took me to these bars where they just kept the drinks coming. Ana, my girlfriend, wasn't old enough to come with us, so she stayed at home."

"All right, then what happened?"

"I got loaded. Drunk completely out of my mind, and at some point this girl walks up to me and starts flirting." He swallowed. "I was young, stupid, and drunk, so what do you think happened? I went home with her and woke up the day after in agony. Mad with grief over betraying Ana."

"That must have been terrible," Solomon said, sounding sympathetic.

"Was that girl underage? The one you had sex with?"

"No, she was even older than I was. But when I told Ana what had happened, it all fell apart. She could never trust me again, and before I knew it, I had lost the only girl I ever loved."

"I'm still not sure what this has to do with your conviction." Yolanda was trying to put two and two together but had so far only come up with five.

"You don't understand how heartbroken Ana was. It tore her apart. She stopped sleeping and eating and became a shell of her former self." The story clearly pained him; he was starting to rock back and forth. "I tried to be her friend, to support her, but she didn't want anything to do with me. Understandably. In the end, she figured her only way out was to punish me for what I had done, so she went to the police and... and she reported me."

"Your girlfriend reported you? For what?"

"She accused me of statutory rape as she was only fifteen when we started being together. I was nineteen at the time, and although everything was of course consensual, that's against Alabama law."

"Oh dear..." Yolanda hadn't expected that. Here she was, ready to go hard on a pedophile and grill the living daylights out of him, but now all she wanted to do was hug that twenty-one-year-old boy and tell him that everything would be all right. Tyne's inexperience had led her to describe this man as a pedophile, but that simply was not the case. Yolanda now, more than ever, regretted not reading through the file before jumping out the door.

"I felt so guilty about the whole thing that I just took it. I barely defended myself in court and of course ended up getting a stiff sentence. I loved her so much, and truthfully... I still do."

"Have you tried contacting her again? After you got out, I mean?" Solomon, ever the believer in true love, was of course trying to find his happy ending.

"No. I couldn't bring myself to disturb her. After I had been inside for a bit over a year I received a letter from her. She said she was doing better and asked me to forgive her for what she had done. I just… I just didn't feel there was any use in replying. I had broken us, and there was no turning back from that."

Yolanda knew that this man was not the one keeping her girl in his cellar. It was not only that he had told a convincing story, but everything else as well. He didn't seem bothered by their visit. He wasn't trying to rush them out. He didn't seem to have a basement. He had immense patience if his ship was any indication, and her instincts told her he was too genuine to do such foul things to another human. He wasn't Mister Whiskers, and he didn't have Lily. They were on the wrong track, and if they didn't hurry, they might never find the right one.

I've been sick for a few days. Mister Whiskers says I have the flu, and he doesn't really want to come near me for fear of catching it. He claims that I didn't get it from him since he hasn't been sick, but I don't know where else I could have gotten it from. He's been accusing me of secretly meeting other people, but it isn't true. I don't know how I would go about doing that when I'm locked in here without any method of communicating with the outside world.

Every time I see him, he'll start with the accusations again. I don't know what to say to that, so I hide under my blankets until he's gone. Thankfully, he never stays long these days because he says I'm contagious, and he claims he can't afford to get sick right now.

When I got sick at home, it wasn't all that bad. My mom would bring me popsicles, and Dad would read me my favorite books. He used to sit with me all day and read and read until I fell asleep. I'm sure he read for hours on end, and it always comforted me. I had two books that I liked the most; they were my "I'm sick" books. Both were by the same author, about this very big house on top of a mountain where there lived a variety of fun beings.

In the books, two of the girls were best friends and always whispering to each other. They did it so much that they ended fused together. I found that funny, especially since Susan and I used to whisper all the time too. There was also this man in the story; he lived on the top floor of the house and was so smart that his head became enormous. The other creatures had to help him get down the many stairs so he wouldn't tip over or hurt himself. There were some pictures in the books, and I remember looking at the creatures in the illustrations and trying to imagine going to the house and becoming friends with some of them.

I don't have my books now, and I don't have my dad either. He used to say that sleep would cure any cold, so I've been taking his advice and reading Alice out loud to myself until I fall asleep. Alice is not bad, but she's nothing compared to the happy creatures who all had their different and funny personalities. I wish one of them would appear now to tell me that everything is going to be all right, and then they'd sit with me and make me laugh.

I miss laughing. It's been such a long time since I laughed. I don't know why, but I think it's probably because I'm always scared, and it's hard to laugh when you're scared. I'm scared that he'll stop feeding me, and I'll wither away in here. I'm scared that he'll yell at me. I'm scared that he'll hurt me, and most of all, I'm scared that he'll keep me here forever, and I'll never get to see any of my loved ones ever again.

Chapter 10

"Oh, it's good to be back," Solomon exclaimed as he plopped himself down and chugged the half-cold cup of coffee he'd left on his table when he went out to chat with Mr. Price. He hadn't been working as deputy for long, and Yolanda knew he'd need a bit more experience before events like these stopped taking their toll on him.

"Does his story check out?" Yolanda asked, leaning over Solomon's shoulder to encourage him to look it up so they could skim it together. It didn't take them long to confirm it, and she sighed, knowing they were back to square one in the search for their girl. "It's not that I wanted this guy to be a pedophile, and of course I'm relieved that he isn't, but I'm just so disappointed that we didn't find her. I had such high hopes."

"I know. Me too." Solomon nodded in solidarity.

"So, how'd it go?" Tyne was back from lunch and seemed to have kept busy while they were gone—her desk, normally very neat, was a complete mess.

"It went okay, but he's not our guy," Solomon replied sourly.

"Oh, that's a shame, but I come bearing good news!" When she smiled, dimples formed on either side of her mouth, just adding to how adorable she really was. Yolanda imagined that her own daughter would have had similar features. Joshua had the same kind of dimples and bubbly personality as Tyne did. Her heart stung when thinking about him. She still loved that man so much and had been devastated when the only way to resolve their differences was a separation.

"What is it?" Solomon jolted her back from her thoughts and seemed to be encouraged by what Tyne had said, turning a half-circle to face her.

"While you guys were out, I called the police department up north and spoke to..." she scrambled around her table for a small note, "here it is. I spoke to a Detective Rick Matthews. As you know, he was lead on the case." She handed the note to Yolanda with his phone number.

"What did he say?" Yolanda was starting to get curious. Getting a perspective from someone else who'd worked the case might be just what they needed right now.

"He was a bit vague and asked to speak to the sheriff. I told him that wasn't possible at the moment since you were out, so that's why he gave me his direct number and said you should call when you came back."

"Tyne, you said something about good news?" Solomon looked annoyed that his sulking had been interrupted, and he wanted an excuse to get back to it.

"Oh, yes, right. I found this in one of the police files." She withdrew a transcript of an interrogation from a small pile on her desk. "It looks quite sketchy, to tell you the truth, and I can see that the police also made notes about it here." She handed Yolanda another document.

Yolanda read through an interview with one of Lily's neighbors, a young boy. He had been at home when she was kidnapped but said that he didn't see or hear anything. For some reason the police found his story and demeanor somewhat untrustworthy, so they had flagged him as somebody either withholding the truth or blatantly lying.

"But this is just a boy who lives way up in Washington. Why do you think this interview is relevant?" Yolanda asked, not sure why Tyne had taken an interest in it.

"Maybe he actually knows something that could be useful. I mean, let's say he saw the make and model or even the license plate... and if he was lying like they think he was, then that begs the question of why he lied, you get me? In that case, he has to have a motive for it, and I'm just wondering... why would he be lying unless he knows something, and maybe the perp bribed him or threatened him into keeping quiet?" Tyne shrugged.

"It says here he has a sister Lily's age, and apparently they were friends." Yolanda wasn't as excited by this information as Tyne, but there was no harm in following every lead. From her experience, that was often the only way to solve a case. Leave no stone unturned.

"Yeah, and that too. Apparently they played together a lot, sometimes at Lily's and sometimes at Julie's. That's the sister's name," she explained. "It all just feels a bit iffy to me and might be worth mentioning when you speak to the detective."

"All right, thank you for that, Tyne. You've done a wonderful job," Yolanda said as she sat down and got ready to call the detective. She was contemplating what to say when Tyne interrupted her again.

"One more thing—I've finished reading through all of the notebooks, and you've got to read this entry, number 1998. Something's not quite right here." Tyne pointed to one of the last entries Lily had written, and again Yoly wasn't sure why the Coosa County deputy was bothered. Before she could ask, Tyne went on, "It may not be anything special read by itself, but if you read it in order with these," she pointed at an entry from Christmastime and the one where Lily had been let outside, "then it all starts coming together."

"Oh shit, you mean that...?"

"Yes, actually, I do."

I wonder if Mister Whiskers has been on a diet recently, because he's lost quite a lot of weight. He used to be a big man with a large belly, but now I see that the skin around his waistline is starting to sag. I know he tried the Atkins diet some time ago and said that it did him some good, so maybe he started that again.

Since he lost weight, he seems to have less trouble moving around my room. He can even fit through the door to my bathroom now, which is much narrower than normal doors. He always used to fit when first I moved here, but as time passed, he became bigger—and it's now probably been some years since he looked into my bathroom. Thankfully I always keep it neat, or he would have been very mad at me when he went there to inspect.

My ceiling isn't as high as other ceilings, but that's okay because I'm not very tall. I wonder why my room is so strange. Maybe it's because it's in the basement, or maybe it was an addition that wasn't built like normal rooms. Whatever the reason, it seems to be pretty soundproof, as no matter how much I scream, nobody can hear me from the outside.

After I first came here, I used to scream and shout a lot. Once I did it when Mister Whiskers had company. I'm not sure I've ever seen him as angry. He came down, completely out of his mind, but he didn't yell, he just grabbed me, tied my hands and feet together and gagged me so my screams couldn't be heard anymore. Every time he had company after that, he would always tie me up and gag me beforehand. He doesn't do that anymore, though. I guess it's because he knows I'm tired of screaming.

The other day was very weird. Mister Whiskers came to me, and he seemed exhausted. He just crawled into bed with me, not wanting to hurt me like he normally does. He then put his arms around me and held me tight, cuddling me till I almost couldn't breathe. I don't know why he did that; he doesn't normally do it, but I really didn't like it. When he hurts me, it doesn't last so very long, and I always have my stars to keep my mind off it. That time the cuddling lasted a very long time. I think it might even have lasted the whole night.

I heard him coughing through the night, but I didn't dare ask him if he was sick or if something was wrong. I know I'm not allowed to ask that. I just pretended to sleep and tried to look at my stars without moving too much. After he finally left, I took my sheets to the bathroom to wash them, like I always do. I don't like the smell of cigarettes or alcohol in my bed. That's when I saw it. First, I was afraid my blood had started again, and I quickly looked at my underwear, but there was nothing there. Later I realized that the blood was also on my pillow case.

It wasn't a big red spot or anything like that but more like small crimson dots all over. Like he had sprayed blood on my bed. I think it's definitely blood, although I have no way of checking it, but it looks like it. Those dark red spots that are almost circular but not quite, just a little squiggly. I wonder if he had been hurt when he came to visit me or what happened. Maybe he had been in a fight? I don't know what to do. It's probably nothing to worry about, but it still makes me uncomfortable. I don't want anything bad to happen to him.

Chapter 11

"Good afternoon. My name is Yolanda Demetriou and I'm calling from the Sheriff's office in Crowswood, Alabama." She waited for an acknowledgement before continuing. "I have some news regarding a missing girl, her name is Lily Daniels." She could hear some commotion on the other side, as if Detective Rick Matthews were sitting up in his chair.

"The Daniels kid? The one who disappeared almost a decade ago?" the man answered, with sincere surprise in his voice.

"Well, a bit over seven years, but you're right. It's that girl."

"What? How? And you said Alabama?"

"I did. The town of Crowswood, Alabama to be precise." She started telling him the story of the skating boys and the notebooks. She then went over the most important facts about the notebooks before finally telling him about the arrival of the father and how helpful he had been.

“Whoa, you guys move fast. So you’ve already gotten the father involved?”

“It was of his own volition. I only meant to do a short interview over the phone, but he insisted on coming down here and meeting up with me. Said anything to do with his daughter would be something he handled in person,” she explained.

“That sounds like Peter. He always was a hands-on kind of a guy. Probably has something to do with his business and the way he conducts it. But all right. You’ve obviously brought us a great deal closer to finding her and figuring out if she’s still alive. This case not ending with a dead body wouldn’t be much short of a miracle, I’d say.” He let out a nervous laugh, obviously not having expected this news when he got out of bed in the morning.

“We believe she’s still alive,” Yolanda corrected him. She put her next sentences together carefully so as not to give away too much and lose control of the case. “We’ve managed to read through all of the notebooks, and we’ve come to the conclusion that her captor is ill. We’re not quite sure what he has, but it’s highly possible that it’s lung cancer, seeing as he’s a smoker and was coughing up blood.”

“You mean he’s dying?” Matthews sounded taken aback.

“We believe so, yes. Not only did the coughing throw us off, but she also describes him intimately cuddling her. That didn’t seem to have been common in their relationship, and then there are those notebooks. Why would he suddenly get rid of them? And on top of that...”

“Yes?”

“He took her outside. Let her sit in his yard.” She enunciated every word, making sure to leave a lasting impression on the man, hoping he’d be inspired to put his resources on the case.

“Oh, dammit, no. Christ, do you think he’s giving her the chance to see the sky one more time before he...”

"I suspect so, yes. We are obviously in a very big hurry."

"All right, I've got this down. I'm going to contact the FBI, since this is crossing state borders and all that, then I'll get myself down there as well. Would you mind if we used your offices?"

Yolanda was surprised by his quick reaction and glad that he hadn't suggested throwing her team out of the investigation. A sudden spark of excitement grew in her belly, pushing forth the belief that they would solve the case and find the little girl. For some reason, she was certain that she'd be a big part of it. She didn't really know why, but she had this gut-wrenching feeling that without her involvement, Lily would never be found.

"Our offices are quite small, but you're welcome to them. I'll call out for some pop-up desks and chairs." She was now smiling, feeling new drops of confidence starting to trickle within her.

"Good. I see it's about a twelve- to thirteen-hour drive, so I'll have to get to it. Rally the troops and then I'll contact the FBI on the way. I'm sure they'll fly in on their private plane fueled with government money. You know how these guys operate."

She did know about the abundance of funds allocated to the FBI as opposed to the small sheriffs' offices and police departments in the country. It was obvious Detective Matthews was joking around with the private plane, as the FBI always flew commercial, but she didn't want to correct him. She didn't have a dog in this fight and would therefore stay neutral, a complete Switzerland, not stepping on any toes. "You know, you could also fly in. It shouldn't be so very expensive."

"Oh, god no. I've got boxes upon boxes of files regarding this case that I'm planning on bringing along. I wouldn't want to risk the airlines losing something important that would be the key to this case. Lost my entire baseball card collection once—never trusted an airline with anything important since." She could practically feel his disdain over the phone.

"That's smart." She let off a breath, but couldn't quite manage a proper chuckle. "I guess I'll see you..."

"Tomorrow morning. I'll head out in a couple of minutes. My wife works from home, so I'll just need to give her a heads-up, but other than that, it'll be fine." He coughed. "You know, this was my first missing person's case. And I've..." he sounded embarrassed, almost shy even, "...I've never really stopped thinking about it. Every year I look over the files again, trying to find something that I've missed."

"And have you?"

"No, nothing yet. There's this one kid we interviewed who's been bothering me, though. His account was just so very—well, I'm not sure how to put it—off? It was as if he knew something but didn't want to say."

"That's odd. Especially since he lives up there, and the perp seems to be from these parts." Tyne's intuition had apparently been on point, as it seemed the detective was mentioning the same kid who had caught her attention.

"Yes, now it doesn't really make any sense, but since I'm opening the case wide up, I'll send a unit over there to talk to him again. See if they can shake him down. I know just the woman for the job. She can get the worst kind of customer to sing like a canary."

Yolanda was pleased to hear that he spoke fondly of a female officer. "Sounds great. Oh, one more thing before I let you go."

"What?"

"Would you mind asking your FBI friends to get a list of everybody with lung cancer in a fifty mile radius around Crowswood and email it over? I'm sure they'll have an easier time with getting the warrant than we would, and then we can start knocking on doors while we wait for you to get here."

"Not a problem. I'm on it. See you tomorrow, Yolanda."

"See you."

Little girl, funny girl
Trapped in a windowless room
You like to twirl and sometimes whirl
As he lurks away in the gloom

You once were free, rid of him
Those days are sadly no more
You still have hope, though fate is grim
Praying that good things are in store

You miss your dad, you miss your mom
Even your silly little bro
Thought your heart is broken and your feelings are numb
You'll soon be rid of this foe

I know it's a silly poem, but I still recite it every day. I composed it when I got here, and whenever I say it, I pray it comes true, that somebody comes to rescue me and take me back to my family, where I can become me again. Down here I'm not me, I'm a part of him. I'm only what he wants me to be. In the back of my mind, I can still hear myself. She sometimes whispers to me, telling me to stay strong, and she says she's waiting right here along with me. She's sure we'll get out, and if it isn't today, it'll be tomorrow, she says. Just be patient, Bonnie, Lily's not gone.

Chapter 12

"How many are there?" Yolanda directed her words at Tyne, who stood by the fax machine, shuffling the paper it was regurgitating into some semblance of order. The FBI had preferred to fax the information over as it was sensitive information and computers could be hacked.

"I think we've got about fifty names so far, but they keep on coming."

"Shoot! This is going to be like looking for a needle in an acupuncturist's trash barrel. How in the world are we going to get permission to investigate the cellar of every single person? 'Hello. How are you? Since struggling with cancer just isn't painful enough, would you mind if we search your cellar for a missing girl?' This is going to be impossible." Yolanda exhaled as she looked through the first two pages Tyne was holding in her hands.

"Thankfully, they sent us not only their names but also their ages," Tyne responded. "That will help us narrow it down a bit."

Solomon pointed at his screen with an index finger as he read out the facts. "I think you might be right about the guy having found out that he's dying. According to the American Cancer Society, the odds of surviving five years with lung cancer is only 18% as opposed to about 99% with prostate cancer. Geez, I'm happy I don't smoke."

"I'll say! I'm sure five years is even long in some cases, it all depends on at what stage the cancer is discovered. Can you see how many people are diagnosed with lung cancer every year in Alabama?" Yolanda sent the fax machine a worried look as it still hadn't finished munching its way through the paper tray.

"It's at just about 4000 new cases every year and with only 18% of them surviving after five years, we can use that to estimate how many people we'd have to investigate according to the area you defined…" Solomon opened his Excel spreadsheet and hammered in some numbers, talking out loud as he did. "So we're looking at 16% of the state, and that gives us about 1600 people, but as we're only looking for men, which are the majority..." He went back to the American Cancer Society's webpage to get the statistics based on gender, "...that would mean around 797."

"797 men?" Yolanda frowned, knowing full well that it would take weeks, or even months, to visit so many homes, even if they were to get help from the FBI.

"Yes, ma'am. But those are only rough calculations, so I might be a bit off."

"That head of yours sure is screwed on right," Tyne said as she approached them, with the final papers from the fax machine in her hand. "Here they are, the whole 813 men with lung cancer within fifty miles of Crowswood." She placed the pile on Solomon's desk with a theatrical flick of the wrist. With wary smiles, they started going through them.

"It's hard to estimate Mister Whiskers' age, but if she considered him an adult seven years ago, he would have to have been at least been thirty then, don't you think?" Yolanda said as she highlighted some names on her papers.

"I guess so, but somehow I always imagined him to be older," Tyne said. "More like forty-five when he got her and in his fifties now."

They all seemed to have had similar ideas but decided it wouldn't be wise to eliminate anybody currently between thirty-five and seventy. As most people with lung cancer were sixty or older, they could eliminate a decent part of that list. After thoroughly examining each and every one, they ended up with 447 names.

"Now that's better," Yolanda said. "Can we narrow it down any further?"

"Well, I reckon he's not likely to be a family man," Tyne suggested.

"Maybe we can look into truck drivers?" Solomon added.

"It is possible he's divorced, but I agree—he definitely does not have a loving wife, kids, and a golden retriever. I'd say it's also likely that he lives in a house or at least in a large apartment with a basement." She paused a moment, biting the inside of her cheek in thought. "Regarding the truck driving, did you find any information about what kind of vehicle was used in the kidnapping?"

"Not really." Solomon went over to the table they had filled with notebooks and examined the index Tyne had put together detailing the contents of each chapter. After some searching, he found the entry about the day of her disappearance. "No, it could be any kind of truck she had to climb up into. Even a big jeep." He seemed disappointed in his lack of progress, if his grimace was any indication.

“Well, we have a start, so don’t beat yourself up over it. Why don’t you go to the county’s Registry of Deeds and see if they’ll give you plans for the houses that have basements while Tyne and I put our internet stalking skills to good use and see whether these poor men have families or not.”

“Ooh, can we go on social media and send them messages pretending to be somebody else and get information that way?” Tyne’s eyes sparkled as if she found the idea quite amusing. “I could be this lonely girl looking for a date, and you could be a divorced cougar wanting a good ol’ time.”

“I don’t think that will be necessary at this point. Let’s just stick to the databases we already have access to and see where that gets us. Solomon, you’re such a Tasmanian devil on that computer, would you mind also checking their marital status while Tyne and I try to find out whether these men have children and live alone?”

“No problem, ma’am. I’ll get some doughnuts on the way; we have to play the part, you know.” He winked at them.

“Way ahead of you.” Lily’s father was standing by June’s empty table, holding a box with fresh doughnuts. While she and Solomon were working on this case, Yolanda had asked June to take care of any local small matters. June had her office phone on divert as she drove around town, saving cats and solving neighborhood disputes. She was very happy with the change from the admin position, as the temporary promotion would give her a lot of experience.

Truthfully, Yolanda was hoping she could make some alterations around the office after the case had been solved, one of those being that June would become a bigger part of their everyday work, and she herself could be more in the office and less out in the field. But that was a headache for another day. For now, it was back in the trenches, and despite not being overly fond of all the different data management chores, she was willing to do almost anything to save Lily.

Lily Daniels
lily!
LILY
LILY!
lily
lily daniels

Chapter 13

"What about this one?" Solomon was driving while Yolanda sat in the passenger seat, scouting the houses from the list. As June was out attending to some kids spray-painting a wall by the local train station, Tyne had to stay behind to hold the fort and couldn't join them on the hunt. Solomon had been able to acquire plans for only a few of the buildings, and the girls had eliminated some names during their investigation. After cross-referencing all the information, they had managed to shrink the list by quite a few names, but that still left them with a bit over three hundred potential suspects.

Solomon and Yolanda had then created a plan of the most sensible driving route before heading out to have a look at the houses—or stalk the owners, as Tyne liked to call it. The current house was the fifth on their list, a one-story brick-and-mortar with black window shutters and a roof that seemed in need of some repair.

"I'm not sure about this one. I think it's possible it might have a cellar, but it's always hard to tell. Let's ring the bell and see." Yolanda stepped out of the car and approached the house. Their M.O. was for Solomon to remain in the car and keep watch while Yolanda went knocking on doors. She was to keep it short and not enter, allowing them to cover more ground more quickly. Just as she was about to cross the street, she saw one of the mosquito spray trucks approaching and instantly dodged back inside to prevent being covered in repellant.

"Have they already started spraying for skeeters?" Solomon said, surprised. Mosquito season was apparently afoot, and when the pesky insect population reached its high point, the municipal government would send out pickup trucks that sprayed pesticide around the neighborhoods to thin the bloodsucking herds.

"Truck's gone, I'll try again," she said after giving it a few minutes for the bug spray to dilute in the air. She didn't particularly enjoy bothering people, especially when it was highly unlikely they had anything to do with the case, but she knew this was their best option.

She rang the doorbell and waited a moment, listening. When she didn't hear anything from the other side, she tried again before walking around the house, attempting to see whether there were any basement windows in the back. As she went into the back yard, she saw a swing set at one end and children's toys spread about. There was a shovel and a bucket as well as an inflatable swimming pool and two dolls stacked on top of one another inside a pull-along wagon. There were also basement windows, and a part of her hoped she had the wrong house, that this guy hadn't found a new victim already.

The back door opened, and a little girl in a pink dress peeked outside, halfway hanging on the door handle. “Who are you?” she asked as she looked Yolanda over.

“I’m Sheriff Yolanda, and who might you be?” She took a step closer, but the child didn’t seem to like that and partly closed the door, peeking out through a small slit.

“I’m not supposed to talk to strangers,” she said, obviously a bit scared of this unfamiliar lady standing in her back yard.

“That’s absolutely correct. You shouldn’t speak to strangers, so I’ll be on my way now, but just before I go, can I ask you a couple of questions? I promise not to come any closer.”

“Well... I don’t know. Maybe?” The little girl was hesitant.

Yolanda decided to just give it a try and hope the child would follow her lead. “Do you live here with your mommy and daddy?”

“Yes. Daddy is at work but Mommy went to the store to get some apple juice since we were out. She said she would only be a minute, and I was watching *Dora the Explorer* so I didn’t want to go with her.”

“*Dora the Explorer* is such a clever little girl, don’t you think?” Yolanda smiled toward the little girl. “What’s your name, sweetie?”

“I love Dora. She’s my favorite.” Her enthusiasm over the cartoon character caused her to open the door a bit more, swinging it back and forth as she spoke. “I’m Lily, and my little brother is David. He’s not here, though; Mom took him with her to the store because he’s only a baby,” she replied, pride at the title of big sister shining through. Yolanda’s heart took an extra beat at hearing the little girl’s name, but she knew this was not the house they were looking for, and she’d better get going before the mom came back with a multitude of uncomfortable questions. She ended the conversation on a polite note, bid the girl farewell, and slowly backed away before turning around to leave.

Back in the car, a look at their route showed the next closest house a few streets away. They were in luck, as the owner was just coming home from a walk, or a ride, as he was bound to a wheelchair. A smiling nurse pushed him toward his porch and up the wooden ramp that had likely been added to the premises after he took ill.

"Not this one, I guess," Solomon said and drove on. "Of the eight we've already visited, how many did we manage to rule out?"

"Only five, and we've already spent close to four hours on this." She replied, feeling her heart sink as she did. They still had way too many names to go through, and time was running out. She needed to figure out a way to either pick up the pace or limit the number of places they needed to investigate. She wasn't sure what she would do, but she was going to discuss it in the morning when Detective Matthews arrived. A fresh set of eyes often brought a new perspective.

Chapter 14

"Have the bureau boys gotten here yet?" A man in his early forties had just arrived, holding a big brown box in his hands, with a laptop case swinging nonchalantly over one shoulder.

"No, they haven't. I take it you're Detective Rick Matthews?" Yolanda responded, barely looking up from the documents on her table. It was only seven-thirty in the morning, and she had come in early to get some work done before the others showed up.

The man nodded, approaching her and placing the box momentarily on the corner of her desk while balancing it with his knee and offering her his hand. "Just call me Rick. These are the files I mentioned on the phone." He patted the carton in question on the side, while simultaneously shaking the sheriff's hand. "Where would you like them?"

Yolanda had wrangled a desk from storage, some Scandinavian monstrosity, and placed it next to Tyne's. She pointed it out to the new arrival. "You can use that desk. I'm sorry we don't have any of those fancy standing ones that you can move up and down and to the sides and what-not, but I hope it will suffice."

"Of course, what do you take me for? Some city clown?" He laughed. "I was raised in the country, on a farm. I just moved to the city after graduating from the academy."

She realized that his presence made her comfortable. His whole demeanor was somehow extremely friendly and nonchalant, reminding her of Joshua and the reason she had fallen for him. Not that she had such feelings for the detective, but it was nice to be around something familiar during an investigation like this.

"What happened with the interview you spoke about? The one with the boy?" she asked.

"Oh, yes. Well, Carmen spoke to him, and after a round of her thumbscrews, she got the boy to admit to having been smoking marijuana at the time of the abduction, claiming that's why he was reluctant to talk about it." He hesitated, "One thing that still bothers me, though, is that she said he wasn't ashamed of the smoking, he just didn't want to tell us because it was none of our business."

"Yeah, that sounds a bit aggressive."

"Back then, I wondered if I'd be booking this kid for something else later on, but he's already twenty-one so I guess he'd have done something bad by now." He shrugged.

"Well, either that or he has never gotten caught," she added. "So, to get you up to speed, what we've been doing is going over the list of cancer patients, putting effort into narrowing it down as they were just about eight hundred when we began."

"And what criteria do you guys use to narrow it down?"

"We mostly use what Lily has described herself, not putting

too much stock into what he has told her, as that could easily be lies. From all that, we've approximated the age of the perpetrator and excluded any building that we know for sure doesn't have a basement." She showed him their list with the exclusions crossed out. "Tyne's going over the medical reports, excluding everybody who was diagnosed this year, as our information indicates that he was extremely agitated during Christmas, and we suspect that's when he either found out he's terminal or was diagnosed."

"But can you be sure of that?" He sounded skeptical on that point.

"No, we can't really be sure of anything, but we need to narrow down that list as much as we can, as we have reason to believe he's planning on killing her." She knew she probably came off as overly severe, but she needed him to either be on board with their plan or give her a great counter argument for doing things differently.

"I gotcha," he replied. Walking over to the stacks of notebooks. "These are all her writings, then?"

"Yes, those are the books that got the case going."

He flipped through one and noticed the fingerprint dust. "Good job with dusting them. I thought you guys didn't think about such things." He winked at her.

"What do you take me for? Some country clown?" She winked back. "I got some detective training back in the day, and while I didn't know early on if dusting them was necessary, I felt it better to be safe than sorry." She smiled.

"Damn right!" He was reading something and seemed a little distracted. "Oh god, this is terrible. Jeez, I feel like everything that happened to her is my fault. I should have found her when she went missing." He looked up from the book, his eyes showing a genuine display of emotion.

"You did everything you could, and what's most important is that we find her now, so put your detective thinking cap on and tell me how we can do this whole thing faster. Our list is way too long as it is."

"I'll tell you what. I'm sure when the FBI gets here, they'll just start raiding houses, so if there's a cellar, they'll find it. But it's still going to take them some time. How about triangulating the patients' phones and seeing which one of them was in Washington at that time?"

"It's a good idea, but I don't think it works, since people change numbers all the time and some numbers might even have belonged to somebody else back then. Then we can't even be sure the guy had his phone with him on this trip." She didn't mean to be negative, but they didn't have time to waste on dead ends.

"Yeah, you're right. It's a shame, because I have the perfect guy for the job. Our tech guy might come off as a slice of pie short of a picnic, but he is just amazing when it comes to these things. Do you think our perp has a history?"

"To be honest, I'm not sure. The worst scumbags don't get caught before they've already managed to do way too much damage." Her mind wandered to the terrible case she had read about in Europe where a man had trapped his daughter in the cellar for over decade, repeatedly raping her, resulting in them having seven children together. It was only when the daughter's eldest child fell ill and needed to be hospitalized that she broke free, or she would have remained in captivity forever.

"I've got it!" He jumped to his feet and started digging into the files he had brought along. "I remember, there was this kid, this autistic kid who said he had seen... wait..." He flipped eagerly through some papers, putting one folder to the side and picking up another one. "Here it is. A boy named Jasper said he saw a red jeep drive by his house. He was looking out the living room window, doing math with the license plate numbers when he saw it, but it drove too fast for him to be able to get more than two numbers from the car's plates. 74 was what he remembered. We had already run that against our DC licenses, but if the guy's from here, no wonder we didn't find him."

"Can your tech guy maybe run that against our list?"

"He sure can—just give me a second and I'll call him!"

Chapter 15

"Oh, hi," Tyne called out from the entrance, wasting no time in going directly to the detective to introduce herself. "I'm happy to see you're settling in nicely."

"Thank you. Are you the lovely lady who organized the notebooks? I've been going through your notes, and they've been extremely helpful in getting me up to speed without having to read through everything." He pointed at the wad of notes that had unmistakably been written by a woman, as they were meticulously systematized and color-coded.

"Yes, that would be me. I finished going through the medical reports last night and have managed to exclude fifty-three more from the list."

"That brings us down to...?"

"Around two hundred and fifty," she replied, her face making it abundantly clear that there were still too many names.

"Okay, that's great. You've done a good job. If we manage to exclude that number every day, we'll have found him before the weekend." He smiled.

Yolanda listened to their conversation and enjoyed hearing him encourage the young woman. It was often hard to get praise in the workplace, even though few things were as important for maintaining good morale. She could very well envision working alongside Detective Matthews and was sure their collaboration would be both pleasant and effective.

His phone rang and he excused himself to take the call, walking out of earshot. Solomon wasn't in yet, but that wasn't unusual. He was one of those guys who showed up late but worked until even later. She didn't worry about it too much, as he was a very valuable and reliable member of the team, and often when he wasn't there before noon, he'd end up bringing in some dramatic revelation that would crack cases wide open, adding in a pecan pie to smooth things over.

"We've got a problem." Matthews was back from his phone call and evidently unhappy with results of the conversation.

"What? What's going on?" Yolanda was surprised at his tone, and she saw that Tyne had moved closer, wanting to get the news the instant it was available.

"That was Eddie on the phone—"

"Eddie?" she interjected.

"Yeah, Eddie the tech guy I told you about, from the station."

"Right. And what did he say?" She put down the paper she was holding, saying a silent prayer that the next thing out of Matthews' mouth would be the address of the monster holding their girl.

"He ran the partial plate number together with the list of cancer patients and..."

“Yes?” She half wanted to tell him to move it along and stop keeping them in suspense, but she had only just met him, so being rude wasn’t really an option.

“He didn’t find anything,” he almost whispered.

“Damn! What do you think that means?”

“I don’t know, but I guess that gives us three options. Either our guy isn’t a cancer patient, the kid remembered the number wrong or saw a car completely irrelevant to this case, or third, and what I find most likely, our guy lives outside the defined radius.”

“You mean that the prick drove for miles and miles before finding the old barn where he dumped the notebooks?”

“I think so. Considering how thoroughly he seems to have planned her abduction, I’m guessing we’re dealing with somebody who knows better than leave any loose ends.”

“But that means he could be anywhere, out of state even, and we don’t even have the slightest idea about where to start looking.” She could hear her heart pounding a mile a minute and desperately wanted to scream at the top of her lungs. This wasn’t happening. It couldn’t be happening. They were losing the girl, and this time, it felt like they were losing her for good.

Chapter 16

Yolanda stepped outside. She just couldn't take any more of this horrible case that was starting to consume her from the inside. How in the world was she going to find that little girl now, when every lead they had just disappeared like a rabbit in one of Lily's magic shows? Falling back on old habits, she did what she had always done in a state of complete and utter confusion—she called Joshua. She knew she shouldn't, as they were separated and were supposed to be moving on with their lives, but she missed him. It wasn't only because the detective from DC reminded her of him but because she still loved him. He was after all, the love of her life.

"Yoly, is that you?" Joshua answered, sounding surprised.

"Yeah, it's me." She paused. "Am I calling at a bad time?"

"No, not at all. What's up?" His voice still sounded husky. She had always loved that about him. That radio voice of his made every word somehow softer and sweeter.

"I have a case. It's a bad one," she finally said, not completely sure how to continue and how much she could really tell him without breaking privilege. "It's all going to shit. I don't know what to do." Her voice sounded more desperate than she had meant it to.

"Oh, crap, Yoly. That sounds terrible. Is there any way I can help?"

"No, I guess not. I just... I just wanted to hear your voice," she replied, realizing how strange her words sounded as soon as they came out of her mouth.

"It's good to hear from you too." She thought she could hear him smiling. "I've been wondering—I know it might be a bit frank of me to ask but... would you perhaps like to have dinner with me this weekend? Say Saturday?"

She was so surprised by the request that the only thing she managed to get out was a stream of different queries before eventually stringing a sentence together. "Um, well, yeah. I would love to. Um..."

"I thought maybe we could go to the cozy little restaurant you love so much. What's it called? Pri... something."

"La Primavera," she replied, knowing full well that his understanding of Italian wasn't necessarily one of his strong points.

"Yeah, exactly. Look, I know it's been almost two months since we last met, but I've got some things I'd like to talk to you about and... well... I'd just love to do it in person." His voice went up an octave, as if he was trying to sound friendly and non-threatening.

Her heart took an extra beat. Last time Joshua had wanted to discuss some things with her, he had wanted them to separate, and as they had already taken care of all their shared assets, splitting things up, all the way down to the photos in the photo album, what could it be, other than that he had found somebody else? He was probably seeing someone and wanted that information to come from him first. He was polite like that, but it still burned so much to think about it.

She swallowed, careful not to let her grief be heard. "All right, that sounds good. Let's say Saturday at seven? If something comes up with the case, I might have to cancel, but if not, then I'll see you there."

"See you there. And Yoly?"

"Yeah?"

"It was good to hear from you."

She didn't remember answering him, but now she was just standing there, holding her phone in her hands, so she had either hung up or actually said goodbye. She was utterly confused. On top of everything with the notebooks, Joshua had some news; news that was extremely likely to break her heart and send her down the road of cuddling her duvet and watching horror films until she passed out from eating too much of her mother's cooking. For some reason, chick-flicks just didn't do it for her. Those classic horror movies were what kept her going.

"Excuse me." She almost jumped as she felt somebody lightly touch her shoulder. When she turned around, she saw two men and a woman dressed in black suits, and she instantly knew that the FBI had arrived—or the Men in Black including a woman, whichever—and those three meant business.

"Are you the..." she started.

"The FBI, and I'm Agent Montello," the man who had gotten her attention replied, showing her his identification. His colleagues followed suit, all three flashing those three big powerful letters and a small badge with an eagle sitting on top.

"Are you here to crack this case and save the girl?" she tried to sound chipper, but due to the effects of the phone call, felt like she had missed the mark.

"We hope so. Agent Philips here has been incredibly resourceful when it comes to difficult cases and seeing as how she was the agent assigned to this case back in Washington, she'll be a great asset. Agent Johnson is also one of our best agents, with years of experience in kidnapping, ransom and negotiation," Montello replied, pointing to his female and male companions.

"Goodie. Let's get to it, then." She attempted to storm into the station but was met by Detective Matthews on her way, almost resulting in a human traffic collision.

"We need to backtrack, we need to go back and go over everything," he said excitedly, as if he had figured something out, not at all bothered by the near miss.

"Yes, I agree. We'll need to read through the books again," she replied.

"No, I don't mean the books. I mean the whole case. We've been looking at it all wrong. We were always looking for somebody in Washington, somebody who had a convenient connection or would fit the bill, but we didn't go through every single one of the cars that were from any farther away than the neighboring states. We were so very sure that he was local or at most one state over."

"But all the traffic camera data must be long gone. It's been so many years, and how many cameras were there really back then?"

"There were actually quite a few, but unfortunately I only copied what I felt was relevant at the time, and those were the five cameras in the vicinity of Lily's route home from school or routes she might have taken had she decided to be a bit adventurous."

"And you still have that?"

"I do. I was determined to solve the case and hoarded data before being forced to stop working on it. They're in my box. We need to set up a new radius around the barn, a bigger perimeter than before and start our search again with the cancer patients. In the meantime, we also need to go over every single piece of footage of cars from the traffic cameras and look them up, trying to match them to the patients or at least to somebody in your state or neighboring states. We start the search again and change our search point from Lily's path to here, to the old barn."

"That sounds like an excellent plan," Agent Philips interjected. "Johnson will give you a hand with that. One of you guys can fill me in so I can see what options I see in this case, but one question before we start..." She looked at the both of them, her face becoming very serious. "Do you have reason to think she's in imminent danger?"

"Yes," they replied almost in unison and watched as the agent's face fell grim and her teeth clenched in determination.

Chapter 17

"Are you sure one hundred miles is going to be enough?" Yolanda asked as they developed the new strategy, watching Detective Matthews circling the old barn on a map with a bow compass. They were throwing quite a wide net, but she'd also thought that last time, and she was not going to make the same mistake twice.

"I think so... It's hard to imagine him driving more than an hour and a half to dump the books, since that would make it a three-hour round trip," Matthews said, looking up for just a second. He had found a gigantic map at the local bookstore that showed Alabama as well as small parts of neighboring states. It was now hanging on the wall next to the coffee machine, where they could easily access it and peer at the tiny names written all over.

"I agree," Agent Philips said. "We need an area to search or we'll be wandering aimlessly, and that will just be a huge waste of time.

You said she's in imminent danger, so let's start with a hundred miles and see where that takes us. I'll have the guys get a new list of patients together, and perhaps you could ask your computer guy to pair it to the footage you mentioned, as he seems to be quite efficient."

"Of course," Matthews replied.

"And you," she nodded to Solomon, "could you help Tyne there go over the patient files for the new patients, narrowing it down as you did before?"

"Yes, sir... I mean ma'am." Solomon was one military salute away from making a fool of himself before catching himself and stopping mid-motion.

"And me?" Yolanda asked.

"You come with us. We're going to go visit these people, and I have a strict partner policy, so you will go with Agent Johnson. Heck, I'll handcuff your hands together like a pissed-off kindergarten teacher if I have to. You two start at the back of the list, while Agent Montello and I will start at the front. I expect to get the full list in a few hours but for now, let's continue with the list you already had and see where that gets us. I'd like a couple of hours to familiarize myself and the other agents with the case, but then I'd like for us to get going."

"All right, that sounds like a plan." Yolanda was hesitant. Something about the strategy felt off. Maybe because she and Solomon had already wasted so much time driving around the state and knocking on doors, but she sensed it was something else, something she couldn't comprehend, let alone put into words and explain. She just didn't have faith in what they were doing, and it had never really done her any good participating in a process that she wasn't instinctually on board with. She didn't know how to get these feelings across, though. All of them were much more experienced than she was, so her opinion was probably not worth much.

She sat down at her desk, contemplating whether she could possibly come up with another strategy, something that would span a larger part of the state and include suspects that lived even farther out. She didn't want them to go below two hundred miles this time, even though it felt a bit excessive. She remembered Lily writing that Mister Whiskers built houses and in another entry stating that he was an engineer who used math in his job. She knew that he could have been lying to the girl, but these clues felt like something worth following if she could just grasp the right thread. As far as Yolanda knew, all engineers used math, but what kind of engineers built houses?

She knew that she should be discussing this idea with her new colleagues. It was completely against protocol, going behind the agents' backs and not even telling her own team, but she didn't want the FBI agents to shoot down her idea before she'd had the chance to explore it. She felt like she had to do something and decided she'd go about this in a different manner, looking into it as a civilian, not in a sheriff's capacity. Without mentioning it to anybody, she did some quick online research and came up with structural engineering as the likeliest match for an engineer who built houses. She started looking up architecture and construction companies that would have structural engineers on staff. She decided she'd pretend to be looking to have some work done on her house. That way she could easily ask about the employees and their qualifications and potentially go on to look them up from there.

In order to not shirk her responsibilities and training, she was going to use her spare time for this extracurricular activity and not waste any time while at work. As she had already gone through most of Detective Matthews' files and gotten up to speed on the rest, she now had two hours to kill while Agent Philips and the others read through the information, and she intended to use this time to the fullest, making sure to keep her personal moonlighting a secret.

Two hours seemed to fly by while she was head-deep in her unsolicited research, and soon enough Agent Philips was standing by her desk, appearing as if from thin air, asking Yolanda whether she was ready to leave the office. The sheriff was so startled that she knocked over her cup, which luckily was empty of coffee, the only reason all of her papers and documents lived to be read another day. She huffed a quick, breathy chuckle, rose from her chair and nodded at the agent. "Yes, of course. I'm good to go."

Knocking on doors with the FBI was very different to doing so with just herself and Solomon. They just flashed their badges and invited themselves in without any hesitation. Although technically needing a warrant before entering people's homes, they got away with it, using an effective combination of presence and determination—nobody blocked them or told them to piss off. It didn't take her long to realize there weren't as many cellars in the town as she had thought, which was very good news. The FBI was also relatively quick and ruthless in their search, having asked Detective Matthews' computer guy to give them information about whether the owners had any extra property, as well as comparing each suspect to the fractional license plate number they had.

As there were still several houses left from Yolanda and Solomon's original search that had spanned fifty miles, they started with those houses, not wanting to exclude them, even though the license number didn't fit. There could always be other explanations for that. When the clock struck two, she had already been to eleven houses with Agent Johnson, and she was sure the other pair had clocked similar numbers. That meant it wouldn't take them long to finish the list.

Finally feeling hopeful and excited, she went to lunch, almost contemplating giving up on her own little hunt. She decided, though, to finish her list of engineering companies while enjoying a hamburger at one of the local restaurants. She would then send the emails out after going home from work that night, expecting to get a few answers by the next day. Whether it was a wild goose chase or not, it made her feel better to explore other options rather than spending the evening watching reality TV with her mother.

Looking up to the skies through the greasy windows at the burger joint, she made a cross gesture over her chest. It didn't come from religious faith but from respect for her own little girl. The one she'd lost that cold winter day who would never, ever come back nor be forgotten. "This world wasn't for you, my sweet, but maybe, together, we can give the world to somebody else. To another angel, such as yourself. You'll help me, won't you?" she whispered to herself, and a faint smile appeared on her lips.

Chapter 18

"I'm telling you, that guy has something to hide," Agent Montello said as he and Agent Philips entered the office together.

"And because I have the patience of a saint, I keep answering you. For the thousandth time, we have no reason to believe he has any skeletons in his closet. I know you didn't like his lawn décor, but you've seriously got to let it go," Philips replied, obviously getting more than a bit tired of this back and forth.

"I'm not saying the Confederate flag had anything to do with it. He just, he just felt off," Montello persisted.

"But was there anything in his cellar? No, we checked. He was also very keen on allowing us to look anywhere we wanted, so I don't see all this off-ness you speak of."

"Well, yeah, okay. But there's such a thing as hidden compartments, false walls and chambers of secret."

"Of course, and his closet was probably the door to Narnia with his garage leading to Hogwarts. Let's get on with it already. Mr. Macklemore is not our guy!"

Yolanda didn't think it strange for Montello to be upset by the Confederate flags displayed all over the state. They were so frequent that it had been a game of hers and Joshua's to count them all as they travelled, and the one who spotted the most would have to buy the other a beer.

She started wondering why that particular guy had registered in Montello's mind. Not wanting to leave any stone unturned, she sat down by her computer to do her own digging, but a quick check revealed what seemed like an extremely ordinary, lonely guy who was the owner of a local store. One of those small convenience stores that still existed with one owner who worked around the clock. She wasn't surprised that he had never quit smoking with such harsh working conditions, which had undoubtedly been the reason he'd developed cancer. It all seemed perfectly legit... perhaps it was just the flag.

She secretly checked her email on her phone and saw that she was starting to get some replies. Her evening had gone into composing and sending emails to the engineering companies. It was extremely time-consuming, as some had contact forms and others had company emails that were hidden somewhere in the About section or buried in the footer at the bottom of the page. She wondered how people could conduct business this way, forcing their clients to play digital Indiana Joneses just to find a way to contact them.

Once she knew whether this was a fool's errand or not, she planned to let the others know what she was up to, but not just yet. With thousands of engineers in the state, it would be one hell of a lucky break if something were to come out of it. Thankfully, many of the engineers were young people just finishing their degrees, and that would aid in her search as she excluded anybody under the age of thirty-five.

"Guys, we've got a problem." Detective Matthews had just arrived, wearing an uncharacteristically grim look.

"What?" Yolanda knew she could hardly take any more setbacks at this point, but she also needed to know everything possible, even if it meant losing ground on the investigation.

"I just got off the phone with Eddie; he was working on this all night, and neither the partial plate number nor the ones from the traffic cameras match any of the new guys either." He looked exhausted, like a man trapped between hope and disappointment, working on little sleep and drinking coffee that no longer helped. The look on Matthews' face and the collapsed hunch of his shoulders bypassed Yolanda's intellect and went straight to her heart. She realized that this case was personal not only to her; he had been looking for Lily for years.

"I've got another list Eddie might be interested in working on." Yolanda spoke before she could stop herself. "It's not fully fleshed out—I just started looking at it yesterday, but it may be worth taking a glance at. That is if Eddie doesn't have anything more urgent."

"No, no, of course. Let me see."

They went over the names Yolanda had collected and the sheet of companies that she had written to, as well as the immense number she had yet to contact. Meanwhile, the FBI agents continued to work down the list of patients, even those without a connection to the partial license plate number. They couldn't be sure that was relevant.

Yolanda and Detective Matthews decided that Eddie would continue sending out her email template to the other engineering firms, as well as looking up the names she had already gotten, comparing them to the plate numbers. He would then run those names against the list of patients they had. Yolanda had created a fake email account for this endeavor in case somebody might recognize her real name, so she just needed to give Eddie her login information, and then she could be on her merry way with the FBI.

Somewhere inside, there was this glimmer of relief, as if she had made the right decision and set a series of events in motion that would eventually lead to them solving the case. Whether the feeling was real or not, it felt satisfying, and that was more than she could have hoped for on a day like that.

Chapter 19

"Please settle down, sir. We're not here to invade your privacy; we just wanted to have a little chat," Agent Johnson said and motioned Yolanda to stay behind him.

"You get yo' ass off my property, ya hear? Or I'll shoot!" A man in his mid-forties was aiming his double-barreled shotgun at them, huffing and puffing aggressively after finding them in his house. Penny, his adolescent daughter, had moments before let them in to have a look and now stood next to her father, desperately trying to calm him down.

"Daddy, they're the police. You can't aim a gun at the police."

"I can do what I damn well please! This is my house. They are on my property. They're trespassing, and I should shoot them right where they stand." His hands were shaking, and he seemed to be in a rather disturbed state of mind. His daughter had told them she wouldn't been expecting him until late in the afternoon when he normally returned from work.

“Sir, I’m asking you nicely. Put the gun down.” Yolanda could see the agent’s gun in his holster from where she was standing, but he hadn’t had time to reach for it, as the man had come swooping in with his own weapon cocked and ready. Johnson was edging his hand ever closer, and truthfully, she wasn’t sure whether it was the right move, as it might just escalate the situation even further.

It all happened too suddenly. Her radio made a sound, Detective Matthews letting her know that Eddie had found something. Agent Johnson took advantage of the distraction to reach for his gun, only managing to pull it halfway out of the holster before the shotgun went off, forcing him into Yolanda, who fell onto the coffee table behind her, smashing it on impact.

Her instincts taking over, she jumped to her feet and pointed her gun at the perpetrator, ready to take a shot. He didn’t say a word, just put down his weapon, leaned onto the kitchen table and bawled. Yolanda quickly removed his weapon and secured the area, handcuffing his arms behind his back before proceeding to attend to Agent Johnson’s wounds.

Thankfully, the homeowner was a terrible shot, but he had still managed to hit the agent in the shoulder, the spray catching a bit of his torso. She grabbed her receiver and called it in while examining the wounds. She then pulled her shirt off and placed it on the wound, not considering for even a moment that she’d be showing off her bra, putting pressure on it to stop the bleeding while they waited for the ambulance to arrive.

“The ambulance is on the way, as are Agents Philips and Montello. How bad is it?” The concern in Tyne’s voice came through loud and clear.

“Not sure. How long until they get here?”

“Five minutes tops. Are you safe?”

"Yes, we're safe. I've got the gun in my possession, and the perp is handcuffed to a chair. He isn't showing any signs of further violence."

"I didn't mean to... I swear... I just... I was just defending myself... he was gonn... shoot..." she could hear the homeowner say between the sobs.

Shit, what a mess, she thought to herself, hoping the ambulance would get there soon and that Agent Johnson wasn't badly hurt. Looking at the spray of shot, it was hard to say what kind of damage had been done. Considering the close range, she hoped he wouldn't lose the use of his arm.

Time almost stood still while they waited for the other agents to arrive, with the paramedics following close behind. Everything that followed was a big blur. She remembered being edged aside while they took over. Releasing the perp from his chair, Agents Philips and Montello pushed him roughly to the floor and cuffed his hands behind his back before pulling him to his feet and marching him unresisting to their car. Getting out of the way, Yolanda unconsciously took a few steps back, backing into a corridor that revealed the stairs. Penny was sitting on the steps, her face a mixture of shock and terror.

Yolanda exhaled and took a seat next to her, gently stroking her arm. Only then did she notice that a couple of pellets had apparently passed Agent Johnson to find their way into her own upper arm, but she didn't pay it any mind, just sat there, comforting the young woman and telling her it would be all right.

"Is my daddy going to go to jail?" she asked, eyes full of tears.

Yolanda knew the answer to that question. Shooting an FBI agent, even if he hadn't killed him, meant only one thing—prison. She still didn't think this was the right time to tell the daughter, who was obviously in shock and needed to gather her wits before facing the music. She was worried the girl wouldn't forgive herself for letting them in, somehow putting the blame and weight of events on her own shoulders. She decided then and there that she'd do everything in her power to help Penny get through whatever was coming.

"Honey, that's not something we should be thinking about right now. I'm going to help you. No matter what happens, I'll be here for you. You hear?" She looked the girl in the eyes, making sure that she knew those words weren't empty.

"You promise?" Penny sniffled.

"I do promise. Whatever happens, we'll tackle it together. Us girls. Now let's start by getting a hold of somebody from your family. Where's your mama now? Can we maybe give her a call?" She tried to sound uplifting.

"No. Mama's in heaven." She didn't seem very saddened by that fact, which meant that her mother had likely passed away a while ago.

"I'm sorry to hear that. What about grandparents or siblings?"

"There's only me, but I have a grandma in Montgomery. She's really nice. Always bakes me cornbread when I visit." The girl smiled and brushed away some tears from her cheeks.

"Well, let's call her then and see if you can stay with her for a few days while we sort this out with your dad. How about that?"

Penny gave her a nod, and with her help, Yolanda called the grandmother, calmly explaining the situation. The teen packed a few things into a bag while a medic tended to Yolanda's arm as well as getting her a new shirt from her car. When they were both ready, Yolanda decided she'd take Penny to her grandma's, seeing as her car was still parked outside, and she didn't want to hand the kid over to one of the detectives after promising her that she would be sticking by her.

The girl was quiet on the drive, speaking up only to give directions, and they were soon pulling up in front of her grandmother's house, which looked nice and neat. There was a small garden at the front, with flowerbeds and a porch with a rocking chair and a small table next to it. The grandma had white hair wrapped in a bun and wore a blue rose-flowered blouse with black pants. As they arrived, she was crouching by one of the flower beds. Penny ran toward her, hugging her. Yolanda followed after, holding the girl's bag and handing it to the grandmother, who asked her granddaughter to go inside and make some lemonade while she had a word with the sheriff.

After explaining the situation to the older lady and giving her a few moments to grasp what had happened, Yolanda was about to drive away when her phone rang. It was an unfamiliar number, so she hesitated to answer, not feeling up to dealing with a scammer, but as she recognized the number as originating from Alabama, she felt she had to take it.

"Hello?" she answered, questioning.

"Is this Sheriff Yolanda Demetriou?" a male voice asked from the other end.

"This is she."

"Good day. This is Jacob Price. You came to visit me a week ago. I'm the one with the historical models."

"Yes, I remember." She didn't understand why he was calling her, as he had made it abundantly clear that he had nothing to do with the case. She had believed him, and a part of her hoped he wasn't about to crush that belief.

"I'm calling regarding that picture you showed me..."

"Yes?"

"I now remember where I saw it."

Chapter 20

Yolanda swerved onto the highway, resisting the urge to break the speed limit on her way over to the other side of the state, to a town called Butler. It was a small town in western Alabama, a quiet and relaxed place where houses were few and far between.

As she drove, Yolanda thought back over what Jacob Price had said on the phone moments earlier about the picture they had shown him. Apparently he had seen the girl in it before, and that had happened at work. It took him a while to piece it all together because it had been so many years back. At first he thought she was the child of one of his coworkers. During the week since Yolanda and Solomon's visit, he had asked around, showing people the picture he'd taken of it with his phone and not getting anywhere with it. Then it finally struck him. He hadn't seen the girl herself but just a picture of her. A picture that had fallen from a wallet.

He remembered bending down to pick up the Polaroid and handing it back to the wallet's owner. Even at the time it had struck him how unusual it was to see a Polaroid photo anymore—they had been so ubiquitous in his youth. He remembered remarking on the prettiness of the girl; he could even envision the man's face as he received the picture and crammed it back into his wallet. His expression had been one of shame, and that's why the picture had stuck with Jacob. It was so odd that the father of such a beautiful girl would be ashamed, but now he knew why. The man wasn't the girl's father but her captor. Price said he had even wondered why that man had taken such a chance as to carry her photo around. Maybe he was becoming overconfident that he wouldn't get caught, or maybe the urge was just so strong that he couldn't bear to be apart from her, even when he was at work.

Yolanda shuddered at the thought, and she could hear in his voice that Jacob was just as upset by it. He said this man was an engineer. He had come to work on construction of a new loading station and had been there for a few months, administering the project. The only reason Price had spoken to him was because he had wanted to do some renovations himself and had wondered if the guy could assist him, maybe point him in the right direction of where to start. The engineer had been very friendly, had given him loads of great advice, and not for a moment would he have thought this man capable of causing another person harm. He just hadn't appeared that way.

Yoly knew those bastards often didn't seem threatening, and that was why they got away with so many horrible things. Some of the worst serial killers even had wives and children. Hardly imaginable, how heartbreaking it must be for the family to find out something like that about their loving husband or father.

Jacob had really done his due diligence; not only had he remembered where he saw the picture, but he had also asked around for the guy's name, going as high up as the executive director of the company to find out. He had finally gotten the name and called Yolanda the moment he did. By then, he had become convinced that the child in the photo was in serious danger and wanted to help.

With the guy's name in hand, Yoly called Solomon, relaying it to him and asking him to look up the man's address. To her surprise, he already had it. It had turned out he was one of the engineers on Yolanda's list, one who lived just a few miles outside of the defined search radius, and they had just matched him to the partial license plate and looked up his whereabouts. Solomon gave her the address, and as Butler was closer to Montgomery than to Crowswood, she said she'd drive ahead, but Solomon was going to follow suit. He made her promise not to do anything before he was there to back her up—one injured officer was enough for the day.

Yolanda promised but did so only half-heartedly; it didn't take a nuclear physicist to figure out that if she saw a reason to go in, she would. Remembering Jacob's words as she gunned it down the interstate, a cold shiver ran down her spine:

"Be careful, he is a big man and seemed strong."

Chapter 21

Yolanda pulled up to the curb and took a long look at the house before exiting her vehicle to approach it. It was so normal, just like any other house on the street. Neither well nor badly kept, just ordinary. In the driveway was an extremely big jeep, one of those extended monster trucks that were useful when going off road. The man could very well be a hunter, something she'd keep in the back of her mind, not wanting him to pull a rifle on her.

She wondered what she should say to him and how to go about being let in. She quickly thought up a lie, one that would get her in the door. Grabbing an old brochure from a box in the back seat, she left the safety of her car to approach the entrance. The door was painted black with a golden door knocker in its middle, and it looked quite nice—she could easily envision a Christmas wreath swinging there during the holiday season.

She hesitantly tapped with the door knocker, heart pounding in her chest. *Should she have waited for Solomon? Was this madness to go in alone?* She knew it was but didn't want to wait any longer. Lily had been locked in for way too long, and Yolanda wouldn't accept her being there a minute longer than necessary. She heard movement from inside the door and unconsciously placed her hand on her gun, unbuckling the top flap of her tactical holster, ready to draw the weapon if necessary.

The man opening the door came almost as much of a shock as the enticing smell rushing out toward her. He seemed to have been in the process of cooking a stew, which smelled absolutely delicious. Jacob had been right; he was a big man, but she guessed he had been even bigger when he was working on the expansion at the trucking company. The cancer was obviously starting to get the better of him—his clothes looked too big, and his face was becoming hollow.

"Yes, how may I help you?" He spoke with a soft and soothing voice. Very friendly indeed.

"Good afternoon, sir. My name is Ann, and I am the new deputy in the county. I just wanted to talk to you about what the sheriff's office does and how we can be of assistance to you." She pushed a brochure toward him. The brochure was from a "Know how to act" campaign they had run in her own county a while back; it had a picture of the former sheriff on the front page with a big smile on his face. She hoped the man wasn't familiar enough with the local sheriff's personnel to know any better.

"Oh," he accepted the brochure, barely glancing at it. "I'm afraid that I am ill-prepared for guests at the moment. Would you mind coming back at another time?" He smiled, obviously hoping to brush her off and get on with his culinary activities.

"I don't mean to be rude, but I only need one more house to meet my quota for the day. Could you please let me give you the introduction? It doesn't have to take long. Five minutes, maximum." She sent him a pleading look, opening her eyes wide in an attempt at a puppy-dog look.

He mulled it over, flipping through the brochure as he did. "Oh, all right. Do you like stew?" Perfectly natural friendliness seemed to just ooze out of him.

"Oh, I love stew. As a matter of fact, it's one of my favorite dishes!" It almost pained her to play so nice with this man, but she wanted to get in, keep him occupied, and make sure he wasn't anywhere near the girl when her backup came. A cornered animal tended to get desperate, and she definitely didn't want to give him an opportunity to do anything before he was handcuffed and booked.

"Well, come on in then. Just sit yourself down in the kitchen and tell me all about the sheriff's office in our great county."

She wiped her feet on the doormat and followed him into the kitchen. Everything inside the house was neat, almost uncomfortably so. It reminded her of one of those minimalistic advertisements she had seen on TV, except it was homelier—not a bland mixture of black and white but nice lacquered wooden furniture and lounge chairs with quality leather. It was a wonderful home, and even though she despised this individual, she understood why no one suspected him of doing anything bad. He painted the perfect picture to keep everybody in the dark.

The man set the table for the both of them and offered her a beer, which she declined, saying she was on the job and would prefer water. There was a well-established rule against accepting food or drinks from a suspect, and while she wasn't keen on breaking it, in this case, she'd make the exception.

He had a big pot on the stove, and there were already two bowls out, as if he had been expecting somebody, which only verified that she was in the right house. One of those was most definitely supposed to make its way down to the cellar. Still, she pretended not to notice anything and just smiled at him, gratefully accepting the bowl of warm stew.

"Please, go ahead," he said as he sat down and dug in himself.

"Mmmmm... that's a great stew." She struggled not to betray any displeasure with the fact that she was eating his food. The food that he had prepared for the little girl who was at this very moment locked in his basement. Yolanda tried her best not to think about the fact that the girl had to starve even longer because she was now sitting in the kitchen. Mentally forcing herself to hang in there, she thought of her comrades, not far behind her, maybe forty minutes away at most.

"So, what was it that you wanted to tell me about?" He had opened the brochure in front of him, ready to pay attention to the young woman here to educate him.

"Yes, well. It's very important for us in the sheriff's office to raise awareness of the public service we provide. We're here to help you out, and you should never hesitate to call us with any questions or concerns. If you see something suspicious, if you are unlucky enough to be burgled, God forbid, or in case of anything you feel is worthy of reporting."

"That's very nice. So if I need assistance, I can call..."

"Yes, you just call the number written on the bottom of every page in the brochure, and we'll be with you in a jiffy." She smiled, pointing at the phone number listed on the page in front of him and moving her hand in a go-get-'em gesture.

"Alrighty. That's good to know. You never know when there might be need for help from the sheriff." He put his spoon down and stood up. "Do you mind if I get my daughter so you can explain the same to her? I'd feel better if she knew about this, too, straight from the source." He didn't wait for an answer but started moving toward the doorway that was located behind Yolanda.

She nodded, not knowing what to say or think, even. *His daughter? Did this man have a daughter?* Before she managed to finish the thought, something hit her from behind, hard. "Ouch," she uttered and tried turning her head, but then it hit her again. As she drifted out of consciousness, a horrible feeling washed over her. He had made her, and more than that, she had given him more time to react than he otherwise would have if she had just waited in the car. Her own insensible actions might have killed the girl.

Chapter 22

As Yolanda came to, she felt her head pounding like never before. She was lying on the floor on her side, next to the chair she had been sitting on, seeming to have taken her bowl down with her, if the stew smeared on the floor was any indication. She tried to get to her feet but to her horror found her hands bound behind her back. *How long had she been out? A couple of minutes? An hour?* These thoughts were interrupted when she heard some commotion from downstairs.

She pulled her knees closer to her chest and managed to rise by using her elbow, and she clumsily got to her feet. Thankfully the prick hadn't wasted time tying her feet together, or she would have been in much more trouble. She looked around and saw a wooden knife block. Backing up toward the counter, she grabbed a bread knife and started slowly hacking at her restraints while maneuvering toward the commotion.

“I’m sorry, my sweet. I didn’t mean to do this so soon, but my hand has been forced.” She could hear the man’s voice echo from the basement.

A sense of relief washed over her as she realized he hadn’t killed Lily yet—she was not too late and could still save the girl. She gently peeked down the staircase to see the man holding the girl’s arm. On a table next to him she saw, to her horror, her own gun. *Holy shit.* She knew she couldn’t go down, or he’d shoot her before she made it halfway down the stairs. She quickly gave her rope one more swipe and *voila,* freedom.

First things first. She had to take off her shoes to silence her movement. She had an extra pistol in the trunk of her car, but that was too far away, and he’d definitely hear the door if she tried to leave. The adrenaline was coursing through her veins, her mind running at a million miles an hour, trying to find a solution to the situation she was in. She desperately needed a weapon, something that would give her an advantage.

Wondering where a guy like this would keep his gun safe, she slowly made her way around the house. Thankfully, his house was as neat and as uncluttered as it could possibly be, so it wouldn’t be too hard to find it. She checked by the entrance, but there was nothing but a closet. She then went into the bedroom, finding one of the ugliest wooden beds she had ever laid her eyes on and a big mounted deer’s head above it. She secretly wished that the thing had fallen one night, the horns impaling the man in his sleep, but then the girl would have starved to death, so while a gratifying fantasy, it was not a helpful one.

She entertained for a second the thought of taking the mounted trophy with her and throwing it at him, but shook her head at the impractical idea and continued searching. She was careful to open the bedroom closet only halfway when glancing inside but found nothing except men's clothes, while a peek in the nightstand revealed only a single Bible. Kneeling down by the bed, she looked underneath and found what she was looking for—a long wooden box with a lock. *Shit, of course the thing had to have a lock. Where would he keep the key?*

A flutter of a thought rushed through her of a movie she'd seen where people kept important things inside books. *It wouldn't, no, it couldn't…* she went back to the Bible and flipped the pages. A small key hidden inside fell to the floor. *Yes!* She had to restrain herself from screaming in joy before opening the box and withdrawing a shotgun. Alongside it was a box of shells, which she quickly emptied into her pockets, two of them going into the weapon itself.

Moving back to the basement door, she peeked down again and saw that the man was standing with his back to the stairs and holding the girl in his arms, hugging her close as if saying a final goodbye. She looked so small, so fragile, like a beautiful little bird locked in a cage. She had a nightgown on, and Yolanda wondered whether she always wore that or if he had also given her normal clothes to wear during the day. The girl looked up at Yolanda and flinched, her eyes moving in every direction as if she didn't know what she was seeing or what she should do.

"What is it?" The man had clearly noticed, and without hesitating, turned his head toward the top of the staircase, already lunging for the pistol on the table next to him.

"Don't move a muscle," Yolanda said cocking back the hammer of the shotgun and aiming it straight at him. He was too fast. She didn't know how, seeing as he was past his prime and clearly in bad health, but he had managed to grab the gun. He didn't point it at Yolanda but at the girl.

"I'll shoot her if you come any closer!"

Her options were slim. Very slim. Trying for a Hail Mary shot with a shotgun was beyond optimistic, and considering her own experience earlier in the day, where the shooter had been standing even closer than she was now, it wasn't going to work. Still, she couldn't put her gun down because then he'd definitely shoot them both. Her only choice was to try negotiating with him, try to get inside his mind and sway it toward her will.

Her mind frantically raced through her single course on psychology back in the academy, and she recalled distant memories of training rats, and there was something called a bystander effect, where people are less likely to help somebody in need when others are around. *Damn it, nothing of use.* She should have paid better attention and not spent the entire class thinking about Joshua and looking forward to their meetup by the library after school.

"Is this your wife?" she asked, acting all innocent, as if her visit had nothing to do with the girl in the cellar.

He hesitated. Hadn't expected her to say that. And for a moment his muscles seemed to ease, and his shoulders dropped just a tiny bit. "Yes… well, no, I mean… She's my fiancée. Aren't you, honey?" He directed his words toward the girl, who was shaking in terror.

"Yes." She swallowed. "Yes, I am."

"She's just lovely. You make a wonderful couple. I don't understand why you hit me—I'm not here to cause any disturbance." She tried to sound as unthreatening as possible.

"You're not the deputy, I know him. The brochure you gave me wasn't even from this county; the area code was wrong," he said between his clenched teeth.

"Yes, one of the boxes we got was meant for another county, but since the phone number routes all calls to the same place, we've just been using it while going between houses," she lied. "I am in fact the deputy. I've just taken over due to..." She quickly skimmed her memory for the name of the current deputy in the county. She had met him before, so it wasn't as deep down in her memory as she had feared, "...due to Liam's wife having a baby and him taking a few weeks off to be with her."

The man seemed to consider what she'd just said, but he didn't look to be quite on board just yet.

"You know, I noticed you don't have a wedding ring. I hope you don't mind me saying, but I can see that you seem to be struggling with some sickness and perhaps..." she smiled, "it would be nice to get married in case the worst were to happen. God forbid."

"What do you mean?" He seemed interested.

"I mean, I'm ordained and I can marry you. That is, if you'd like. I see the lovely lady's got her dress on and everything, so it would be just perfect." She hoped to play into his possessive nature, which was so evident from Lily's writing; if she managed that, it would buy her some time. Watching the girl's face become stiff, her terror turning into complete revulsion, didn't make this any easier. Yolanda could truly feel for Lily and wished she didn't have to play this game in front of her.

"That's actually..." He was considering it. Yolanda was sure he hadn't thought about marrying the girl before, as he feared she wouldn't comply and would be taken away from him. This new situation was something he hadn't foreseen, and who didn't want to seal the deal before meeting one's maker? "That's not a bad idea. I've got my mother's ring upstairs," he finally replied and started moving toward the stairs, pushing the girl in front of him, the gun still aimed at her head.

Yolanda didn't put the shotgun down, just followed after them as he pulled Lily toward the bedroom, making sure to keep the girl between Yolanda and himself. He was just about to bend around the corner and go toward the bedroom when there was a hard knock on the door. Yolanda's heart skipped a beat. It had all been going so well, and she was just waiting for the right opportunity to make a move. For a split second, her face became completely blank, and she knew everything had just changed.

Chapter 23

Are they with you?" he demanded, and his eyes were shooting daggers.

"No, I don't know who they are." She put up the straightest face she had ever mustered and stared right at him, not a quiver in her voice or expression.

"You mean to tell me that on the same day, there aren't one but two random knocks on my door, and they're not connected? That they have nothing to do with me or the girl?" He didn't believe her, that much was obvious. She needed only one chance to make a move, though… and he needed to make only one mistake that she could take advantage of.

"Yes. I am telling you that. Now are we going to get married or not?"

"What do you think?" he sneered.

At that moment, a small red pointer shone through the window, flickering on the man's body before landing steadily on his chest. Yolanda smiled, unintentionally, but it was enough for him to notice.

"What? What is it? Why are you smiling?"

"Nothing," she attempted, but he noticed the beam.

His eyes opened wide, and he jumped in surprise. "What in the Lord's name—?"

Before he could finish that sentence, Yolanda had barreled into him, grabbing his gun-hand with her left and pinning it down. "Lily, open the front door!" she screamed at the girl, who just stood there, utterly confused, too shocked to move. "Open the door and let them in!" Yolanda screamed again, but the girl stood rooted to the spot. Instead, she just lowered herself onto the floor, pulled her dress over her legs and covered her head with her hands in an instinctual defensive posture.

Yolanda continued battling the asshole, who was still holding the gun. He was strong, but thankfully not as strong as he would have been when healthy. She may not have paid attention during psychology class, but this she was trained for. She got him to the floor with her on top, pinning his gun-holding hand down and pushing her arm toward his throat. She tried to overpower him, but he wasn't giving up. He kicked her in the back with his knees and hit her in the side with his free arm, causing her to flinch in pain. Then somehow he managed to pinch her torso between his thighs, pulling her toward the floor.

Yolanda was quick, though. Swinging her leg toward his gun-hand, she managed to kick the pistol, sending it skidding toward the sofa. He didn't let that stop him but used the opportunity to sit up and jump on her, trying to swing at her face with his fist. She dodged the blow, elbowing him in the chest, but he still didn't stop—just continued beating her while putting his whole weight on her legs.

Her legs quickly became numb from his weight pushing down on them, and in an effort to free herself she turned to the side, throwing his balance and momentarily getting him off of her. He gave her the meanest look she had ever seen before lunging for the girl where she still sat, cowering on the floor. His hands were aimed for her neck, and Yolanda knew what he was going after—he intended to leave no witness to his crimes.

"Noooooo!" she screamed and grabbed his legs with her hands, and to her own surprise, she bit him, right in between the pants and his socks, pinching his Achilles tendon hard between her teeth.

"You bitch!" he howled and turned his attention back to her, fully fixed on getting his revenge.

She tried to crawl toward the gun, but he managed to pin her down again, this time even harder than before. She was struggling to protect her face from his forceful blows; a few of them hit her in the torso. It was a battle to the death, and she knew she had to make a move and do it quickly before he managed to completely overpower her. Sacrificing her face to free one hand, she lunged for the crown jewels, taking a hard hit on the chin as she did. When her hand found the target, she didn't just squeeze. She twisted and pulled so hard the guy let out an inhuman scream. It proved enough; she managed to free herself while he recovered and didn't waste a moment, jumping toward the sofa to get her gun. She was so enraged, her whole body shook, and she just stood over the still howling man, her pistol aimed at his face. She was ready to fire when Solomon burst in through the window.

Chapter 24

"Yoly, NO!" Solomon screamed from somewhere far, far away. She wasn't herself anymore; she wasn't even in this world. She was just alone in a desert with this monster of a man, and she had one up on him. She was the one holding the gun. One pull of the trigger was all it would take to rid the world of this man, to be forever free of him. She had the power to do that. One simple move of her finger. Just a miniscule movement to save her precious girl.

She started slowly tugging at the trigger; she was going to savor the moment, watching him as she did so. Then she felt something grabbing her arm. Something was pulling at her. *What was it?* She zoomed back, and there was Solomon, standing there, pleading with her, his voice cracking. It was as if she had snapped out of a trance, a haze that assured her that all was as it should be—the girl was safe, and Yolanda would exact justice.

"Don't do it, Yoly. You'll ruin everything you've worked for. You're making a difference. Don't let it all go to waste. Please," he pleaded.

For a moment she looked back at the girl, whom Agents Philips and Montello were helping to her feet. They pulled her toward the door and out of harm's way. The girl didn't look happy to see Yoly threatening the man—she looked sad. As if she did not wish for this man to die. Perhaps a natural reaction, having been locked in for so long and allowed to bond with no one but him over so many years. Yolanda hated the man who had made the little girl feel that way. She loathed him. How he could force her to be his to the point where her very heart and soul belonged to him? She wanted to pull the trigger so badly, so very badly.

"Yolanda," Philips was now standing behind her. "Don't do this. I assure you that I will do everything in my power to get a speedy trial and make sure he goes somewhere where child molesters get the proper treatment. It won't even be hard—men like him are persona non grata among even the worst scum."

Philips was right. Being raped in prison would be a better punishment for him, maybe even getting shivved or whatever they did to guys like him. She slowly lowered her weapon, the red fog over her eyes dissipating. The bastard was dying anyways, and it wasn't worth throwing away her whole career as well as the potential of the next woman who might occupy her office. This guy had taken more than his share, and he wouldn't take that too. A part of her hoped the inmates wouldn't murder him too quickly; he didn't deserve such mercy.

The agents rushed toward the man, cuffing him, as Yolanda limped over to the sofa, plopping herself onto it, completely drained. It had been the longest day, from Agent Johnson getting shot to herself almost getting killed, but they had saved the girl, and that was all that mattered. She turned to Solomon, who was sitting on the opposite side of the sofa, grinning, happy with the result.

"Why didn't your sniper shoot the guy?" she asked, confused. It would have saved her quite a lot of grief if they had just taken him out before they'd started an amateur MMA session on the floor.

"Oh, the sniper? It wasn't so much a sniper as it was my son's laser pointer. I found it in my pocket and thought I might as well make an attempt at defusing the situation, you know?"

Yolanda stared at him, eyes wide, and before she knew it, she was laughing her heart out. Solomon laughed, too, and there they sat like a couple of lunatics, rolling around, holding their sides in pain. She knew it was probably the tension and lack of sleep that had been building up since they found the notebooks, but she didn't care. It was good to laugh, and it was even better to laugh with Solomon. She knew she had hired him for a reason—he had this little spark in him, a spark that had just saved the girl's life as well as her own.

"Oh dear, you should check out the cellar he kept her in. Nobody would have ever found that room," Montello said, looking grim. "It's hidden behind a shelf, and the prick just put wheels on it and some hinges so he could move it back and forth as he pleased."

"But wouldn't she have been able to open the door from her side if she'd pushed hard enough?" Yolanda asked, standing up to follow her deputy, wiping a stray tear of laughter from her cheek.

"No, he had a lock on the door as well as the shelf. He then just propped up a hanger where he hung his work clothes, covering the lock entirely. Seems it can be useful to have an engineering degree if you're a child molester." He shook his head, not okay with what he had just seen.

The girl's quarters were very small. About the size of a hotel bathroom. She had a bed and one table, a standing lamp and one for her table as well as a pile of books on the floor. On top of one of the piles lay *Alice in Wonderland,* open in the middle as if she had been reading it. Yolanda picked it up and flipped through it. It was worn, looking like it had been read over a hundred times, the spine almost falling apart. It warmed Yoly's heart that Alice had helped Lily through this, and she placed the book back where she'd found it, knowing exactly what to do next.

Chapter 25

Yolanda made one stop on her way to the hospital. The others had told her that Agent Johnson was awake after his surgery and recovering nicely but would require some physiotherapy to get his hand back to its former state. Fortunately, most of the pellets had missed the agent and Yolanda and had gone into the wall behind them.

Before getting to the hospital, she had spoken to the psychiatrist appointed to Lily's case, who advised her to wait before calling the girl's dad, just until the examinations were finished. They needed to do a rape kit, which was invasive and difficult for the victim, but to build the strongest case against this guy, it was essential. The psychiatrist also thought that seeing her dad after all this time might be too much for Lily to deal with right now.

Yolanda found Agent Johnson in a spacious corner room of the hospital, almost a suite—she wasn't surprised, and a part of her found it fitting, seeing as he had been hurt in the line of duty. He looked well, despite his left hand being in a cast. There were balloons tied to the foot of his bed and a box of confectionery by his side. A stuffed bear was sitting near his pillow, a heart on its chest with 'Get well soon' splashed across it, clearly something that had been picked up at the hospital gift shop and somehow had Tyne written all over it.

"So how the heck are you?" she said as she barged right in and sat herself down in a chair by the bed.

"Not too bad, not too bad. I heard that you solved the case while I was taking a nice drug-induced nap," he said, a hint of sadness in his tone. She imagined that he must have felt left out, not to have been there with them when they caught the bastard.

"Yes, but not without your help. You were a valuable member of the dream team," she replied, attempting to cheer him up.

"I guess." He looked past her out the window.

"Oh, I got you something." She handed him a gift in blue wrapping paper.

"What is it?" He sat up. She had asked the woman at the bookstore not to put any ribbons on it since he wouldn't be able to use both hands. He flipped the gift over with his usable hand and slid his thumb under the tape holding the wrapping paper in place. Removing the gift wrap, he revealed a book, *The Man Who Mistook His Wife for a Hat* by Oliver Sacks. "How did you know?" His face lit up as if it were exactly what he wanted.

"You mentioned something in the car about loving these kinds of neurological mystery books, and after snooping around on Goodreads, I saw it on your want-to-read list." She winked at him. "You FBI guys aren't the only ones capable of some spying."

"That's amazing; thank you so much!"

She stayed with him a while until she got a call from the psychiatrist that Lily was done with all the examinations and that it would be all right to look in on her, though he was very firm that Lily was not to be asked any questions about the case nor pushed for information. She'd need a couple of days before that would be possible.

Lily was looking out the window when Yolanda found her, watching the birds in the trees and the people walking below the building. She looked so happy, so serene, that Yoly wondered whether she should just come back later and not disturb her for now. Quietly placing a gift on the bed, the sheriff was about to leave when Lily noticed her and turned to address her.

"You're the one who saved me, aren't you?" she asked, her voice surprisingly calm.

"I guess I am," Yolanda replied with a smile.

"You're smart," Lily continued, looking Yolanda over. "It was very smart to tell him you wanted to marry us. That gave you more time," she added.

"You're also very smart, realizing that I wasn't being serious. I'm truly amazed how intelligent and strong you are," Yolanda told her, sitting down by her side, keeping her movements relaxed so not to make the girl nervous.

"I wasn't the smartest kid in class, you know," Lily said, reminiscing. "Sometimes, when I was playing around with my friends and not listening to the teacher, he said I was such a disappointment." She smiled, obviously finding it funny now.

"Well, we all change, and often it's not the most diligent children who turn out to be the best people."

"Do you know when I can meet my daddy? The doctor said he was here in town." Her eyes were so big and so very sincere.

The psychiatrist had told Yolanda that Lily had repeatedly asked for her dad, but he didn't want to do anything before confirming with the police. Yolanda had therefore offered to take care of informing the father. She'd asked him to come to the hospital an hour later, when the doctor was available to supervise the visit.

"Soon," she replied. "You can see him soon." She picked the present up off the bed. "In the meanwhile, I've brought you something."

"Is that for me?" Lily seemed utterly surprised, which Yolanda took in stride, since the girl hadn't gotten a proper present from anyone for a long time.

"It is. It may not be much, but I was hoping it would make you a little happy."

The gift had pink wrapping paper with a purple bow and a card. Lily opened the card, which had a picture of a big flower on the front. "It's a lily, just like me," she said, smiling.

To the strongest lady I know.
At your service always,
Yolanda

Lily removed the packaging so very gently, straightening out the ribbon before placing it next to her and taking care not to rip the paper off when removing the tape. When she saw what was inside, her whole face lit up and she stared at Yolanda in amazement, her mouth gaping open. Lying on top of the folded paper was the third book of Tolkien's Lord of the Rings trilogy, *The Return of the King.*

Chapter 26

Yolanda didn't leave until Lily's dad had come along, making her a bit late to the restaurant. It was quite a sight to see their reunion, to see him embrace her and watching Lily as she tried to participate, but having some problems with it. It was as if she had somehow lost the knowledge of how to hug somebody who truly loved her during all those years of captivity. Yolanda knew it would take time, but somehow she was confident that Lily would eventually return to her former self. A thought which, for the very first time in a long time, made her feel optimistic.

When she entered La Primavera, Joshua was sitting at their favorite table, nursing a glass of whiskey. He always drank whiskey when he was stressed about something, and that, in turn, made her even more nervous than she had been before. This was the first time her mind had turned toward the dinner, as she had been far too occupied with everything else up until now.

"I'm sorry I'm late. I had to sit with a young victim and didn't want to leave her," she said as she set her bag down on the floor and took a seat opposite Joshua. He looked nice, in a dark blue shirt with a cyan tie that brought out the color of his eyes. She had always found him handsome, and tonight was no different. He was probably one of the handsomest men she had ever met, and it still pained her that it hadn't worked out between them.

"Don't worry," he said and smiled, already putting her at ease. "They had Glenfiddich, so I'm perfectly fine. Just enjoying every sip of this beauty."

"Have you ordered? I'm starving." She had just realized that she hadn't had any food since morning and desperately craved some of the delicious lasagna the place offered. There weren't many Italian restaurants near Crowswood, so this one had always been a favorite of hers, seeing as she loved all ethnic food.

"No, not yet. Do you know what you want?" He handed her the menu, but she lifted her hand and waved it away.

"I'll just have the lasagna as always."

"In that case, I'll just have the same." He took her in, noticing the bruise on her face. "Honey, what happened to you? Are you all right?"

"Oh, it's fine. I had a bit of a tumble with a child molester earlier. No biggie." He looked shocked, reminding her how much she enjoyed teasing him. "Don't worry. I'm fine. I've been checked out by the docs and sent right back out on the streets to serve our great county."

"If you say so." He didn't seem convinced. "It's good to see you, though I don't enjoy seeing you injured." He reached for her hand out of habit, but when she didn't take it in hers, he pulled back. "I'm sorry. I guess I'm not used to the separation yet."

"No, it's one of those things that takes time getting used to. You said you had something you needed to tell me?" Yolanda was too tired to drag this out. She just wanted to get it over with so she could go home and take a long nap. It was actually a good day for bad news, because this time, it wouldn't keep her up. She was beyond fitful insomnia. A nuclear attack wouldn't disturb her.

"Yes, that. Well... I've been offered a job."

"That's wonderful." She took a bite out of one of the rolls from the basket the waiter had put in front of them. If that was the extent of his news, then this hadn't been anything worth dreading. A new job—did he need to take her out to dinner for that? Why didn't he just tell her over the phone? There had to be more to it. "What kind of job is it?"

"I've been offered a position at a firm where I have the possibility to become partner." He took a deep breath as if preparing to say something she wouldn't like. "The job isn't in Alabama. It's in DC."

"Crap." The word just slipped out. She hadn't meant for such a strong reaction and had been determined to show no emotion whatsoever, but this was not what she had expected to hear. A new girlfriend, yes, but a job and moving far away? No, that she wasn't a fan of.

He smiled at her, noticing that she was embarrassed by her own reaction. "It's so good to see you. I've truly missed you," he said and made another attempt at taking her hand in his. This time she let him. "I don't want this to be over." His face turned sad.

She didn't want that, either, but it just hadn't worked after the accident. After having to come to terms with their baby dying in the fall, and after months of Joshua blaming her for going to work that day. Saying she should have known better than to run up the icy stairs without holding the railing. Yolanda just hadn't been able to take it anymore. He had been so mad at her. Sometimes he hadn't even been able to look at her, and having the love of her life despise her was more than she had been able to bear.

"I miss you, too, but we can't go back to what we had. The accident changed everything."

"I've been seeing a specialist," he said, looking her straight in the eyes.

"What does that mean?" She didn't know what kind of a person he'd call a specialist. When it came to Joshua, it could mean practically anything.

"A psychologist. A guy who deals with loss and anger. I've been seeing him ever since we separated." He looked a bit humbled. "I didn't want to be the man I had become. I was so angry at everybody, not only you. It was like I was carrying this whole big bag of grief on my shoulders that over time turned into immense anger."

"And do you feel better now?"

"I do. Much better. Dave has taught me how to tackle my emotions, something that was neglected in my upbringing. You know how my family is. How closed off they are."

Joshua came from a very nice, tight-knit Christian family, where they had dinner every Sunday after church. The problem was that any issues were always swept under the rug. Yoly had noticed this tendency in Joshua early on but had always hoped that he would learn how to actually address things. Her upbringing had been the opposite of his; as a teenager, she had fought with her mother, and because of that, their relationship became much deeper. They in turn had become able to discuss and share everything. It was something she felt Joshua envied.

"I'm confused. Why are you telling me all of this?"

He reached for her other hand and looked her deep in the eyes. "Yolanda, I want us to move back in together and to be completely honest..." His face became determined as if he were absolutely sure of what he was going to say next. "I want you to come with me to Washington."

Chapter 27

Coming to work the next day was very strange. Yolanda had allowed herself to sleep in and didn't show up at the office until about ten, when she had found Tyne already tidying up with the help of Solomon. Yoly had grabbed a box of doughnuts and some coffee along the way to reward her team for a job well done, but she had hardly passed the threshold when she was received with a grand round of applause.

Detective Matthews was ecstatic to close the case that had been haunting him for so long. He said he'd be heading back to Washington later that day alongside Lily and her father, where they'd start putting together the report. There was still quite a lot of work to do in regards to the case, but the FBI had taken over to speed up the process for a quick and effective prosecution. They had already talked to the prosecutor, who was hoping to push for a plea bargain by asking the judge for a sky-high bail. Philips knew the appointed judge and said he was a hard-ass, one who loathed child molesters. That, as well as the violence of the alleged crime and the fact that he had crossed state lines to commit it, made them optimistic that Lily's captor, Donald Townsend, could be dropping the soap in the shower halls of the county jail while waiting for his trial.

There was one final piece of information that Matthews' team in Washington had shone light on. The kid who had behaved suspiciously, the brother of Julie, one of Lily's friends, turned out to be a nephew of Mister Whiskers—his father was Donald Townsends's brother. Although the parents didn't seem to know anything about it, and nor did Lily's old friend, the son had gotten a very big Christmas present from his uncle that year, which was uncharacteristic. Matthews was hoping that Carmen would be able to squeeze more out of him before the trial and perhaps prove that it was all premeditated, that Townsend had chosen Lily especially and had paid the kid to help him, to keep quiet, or both.

Although Yolanda was pleased that the case was coming to an end, she would miss the people she had made friends with while working on it. Tyne was a sweetheart who worked hard and had her moral compass set due north. Detective Matthews had become a friend of hers, and her relationship with Solomon had become even stronger after all of it. The FBI guys had also been great, and it never did any harm to know somebody on the inside of the J. Edgar Hoover building. All in all, it was a satisfactory ending to a horrible case, something she couldn't even have dreamed of in the beginning.

What Joshua had said the night before was still swirling around in her mind. They had spent the evening and the night together, but she wasn't sure yet whether it was a good idea to reconcile.

He was moving to Washington in two months, and they'd have that time to rekindle their relationship and see where it would take them. Her mother was retired, and the only thing keeping her in Alabama was Yolanda. Her tele-novellas could be watched anywhere, so she'd easily move to DC with them. There was a bigger Greek community in Washington, and perhaps her mother would be happier there, not having to drive over half an hour to attend her Orthodox masses. And seeing as the old sheriff would come back to reclaim his job when he got better, there wasn't very much holding Yolanda here, except the fact that she'd be unemployed if she left. Then again, Joshua's salary would easily sustain them while she got her affairs in order.

She had always wanted to go back to school and finish her criminal justice degree but hadn't seen any reason to, as she was fairly well settled at the sheriff's office. With that degree in her back pocket, it would be easier to get a job as a detective. Perhaps now was the moment to return to the classroom—that is, if she was willing to trust Joshua, and so far she had no reason not to. He always stood by his word, and there didn't seem to be anything he wouldn't do to help her. It would also be easier to be a mixed-race couple in Washington than here, where they attracted uncomfortable scrutiny. Whatever people might say about DC, at least it was the twenty-first century there. Her mind was racing, but so far, it seemed all her thoughts were leaning in one direction.

As she hugged Detective Matthews, or Rick as he preferred her to call him, he told her it had been a pleasure to work with her and that she had the perfect nose to be a great detective—"the kind to get into just the right amount of trouble." He encouraged her to pursue that career, and if she ever decided to try policing in a more urban setting, he'd give her his best recommendation and try to persuade his chief to take her on. "There are never enough good detectives around," he said with a grin.

He didn't know it, but that offer was exactly the flint and tinder she had needed to make up her mind about the future—to decide what to do next and whether it was time to put her khaki sheriff's pants on the shelf and move to the big city. She had always liked Crowswood, but DC was bigger, full of opportunities. Maybe it was even a place where dreams come true, dreams of a big belly and little feet running across the floor to greet their daddy when he came home.

1

Dear diary,

Daddy says this is the proper way to start an entry, so I've decided to always do that from now on. He bought me a pink book with unicorns on it to write in and a pen to go with it. I like it, even if I might be a little bit too big for it. I don't think smiling over some colorful creatures is a bad thing, though, and besides, I've got to make up for all the years I didn't get to watch and laugh at silly unicorn cartoons.

My little brother Bill has become so big. He's almost fifteen. When I disappeared, he was only eight years old, just a baby. Now he's a teenager and loves to object to everything Mom says, though he still seems to listen to Dad. I wonder if it's a guy thing, that the men stick together against the women. I look forward to finding out more as I get to know them better and learn how to be part of a family again.

While we were driving back from Alabama, Dad explained about what had happened since I left. He told me that Grandma Lily had passed away, which made me sad. I've missed her quite a lot, but he said she had been sick and was in a better place now. I'd like to think that she was watching over me and that she's the reason Sheriff Yolanda found me. I'm sure Grandma guided her to me.

I will forever be grateful to the sheriff for helping me and for being smart about how to get me away from Mister Whiskers. Yolanda told me his real name is Donald Townsend, but to me he'll always be Mister Whiskers. The cat is still here, but to my surprise, he's not mean anymore. He still has the spot, though, so I guess my theories about the spot were wrong. Bill says he became nice after we got our other cat, the one called Mister Paws. I guess the cat was just lonely, and that's what made him angry. Sadly, some company didn't make my Mister Whiskers any less mean.

The lady psychiatrist in Alabama told me I would need help getting back on my feet, and she discussed that with my dad. They've found me a very nice woman back here who's going to help me with understanding what happened to me and how to work through it. I like her very much. Her name is Eliza, just like the princess from *Frozen*. *Frozen* is one of the first movies we watched when I came back, since I wanted to catch up on all the Disney films I didn't see while I was gone. I think it's an okay movie, but I suspect I would have enjoyed it more a few years ago. Next weekend we're going to watch all the Ring movies in a row. It's going to take us the whole day, and I think it's going to be great. I've already read the book Yolanda gave me and I loved it. I even think it's my favorite one of the three.

I've told Daddy that I'd like to go back to school, but he says it'll have to wait a little bit. He says he'll do everything he can to help me with that and that we're going to start on Monday, going over what I've missed. Since he works for himself, he can use part of his day to teach me, and I think that's going to be perfect. Just my dad and me studying together. I hope we spend most of our time doing math.

Mom was very happy to see me too. She said she had missed me terribly. She's still a big boss, but now she works for an even bigger company than before. I've decided that I'm not going to pursue magic like I wanted to when I was young but will become like her. My mom has not only power but also grace, and she always knows what she's doing. Dad says I'm beginning to look like her, but I don't see it. I just see a little girl who desperately wants to get back on track with her life.

My friends are very different from how they were when I disappeared. They're all so big now, and some even have cars and drive everywhere. I've already met up with Susan, and she still lives three houses down from me. It was sort of weird, and we didn't really know what to say in the beginning, but then we just started exchanging stories, and it was great. She told me about school, what had happened since I left, and I told her about what had happened to me. Susan became very upset when I explained my life with Mister Whiskers, and said that ever since I disappeared, she had felt guilty for being sick that day. She apparently got sick from kissing a boy, and if she hadn't done that, she thought none of this would ever have happened.

I told her I never blamed her. I blamed only myself for not listening to my parents. I knew I shouldn't have talked to the man. I knew I shouldn't have climbed up into his truck. I should have believed what they told me about bad men with nice faces and puppies. I just hadn't. I was only a child, and this should never have happened to me. But it did, and now it was over. I lost almost eight years of my life, and I am going to make damn sure I get them back by doing everything I want from now on, starting with going back to school and becoming someone great. This will be the life I make for myself, the life I should have had. The one I deserved.

Here is a link http://eepurl.com/dNAXPs
and QRCode to my mailing list.
Feel free to sign up for regular updates on
my future books.

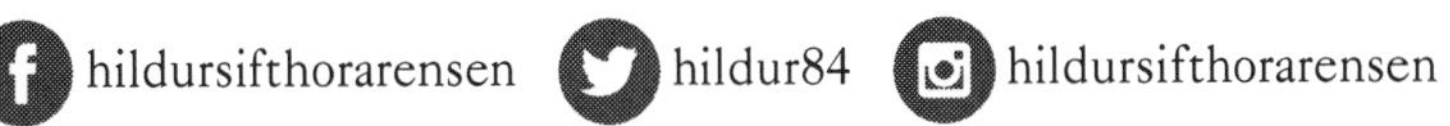
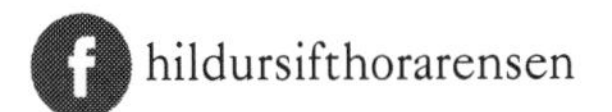

hildursifthorarensen hildur84 hildursifthorarensen

With much appreciation and love to my supportive patron: Julie Caple

Printed in Poland
by Amazon Fulfillment
Poland Sp. z o.o., Wrocław